PRAISE FOR
BENEATH THE BLACK PALMS

"Hardboiled as all get out—no noir devotee will want to."
—Barry Gifford

"Unapologetically confrontational, grimly poignant; a gritty depiction of LA vice and vicissitude."
—*Kirkus Reviews*

"Amazing, beautiful, heartbreaking work."
—Allison Anders, writer/director of *Gas Food Lodging*, *Border Radio*, *Mi Vida Loca* and *Grace of My Heart*

PRAISE FOR NOLAN KNIGHT

"Knight's slangy prose is a perfect fit for characters whose dreams die slowly or explosively."
—*Publishers Weekly*

"*The Neon Lights Are Veins* is a dope-fueled gutter-punk odyssey through a gaudy nightmare version of Los Angeles. With echoes of James Ellroy and Nathanael West, Knight carves out his own bit of L.A. crime-writing turf in this impressive debut."
—Richard Lange, author of *Rovers*, *Dead Boys*, *This Wicked World*, *Angel Baby*, *Sweet Nothing* and *The Smack*

BENEATH THE BLACK PALMS

BOOKS BY NOLAN KNIGHT

The Neon Lights Are Veins

Collection
Beneath the Black Palms

NOLAN KNIGHT

BENEATH THE BLACK PALMS
STORIES

Down & Out Books
3959 Van Dyke Road, Suite 265
Lutz, FL 33558
DownAndOutBooks.com

The characters and events in this book are fictitious. Any similarity to real persons, living or dead, is coincidental and not intended by the author.

Cover design by Margo Nauert

ISBN: 1-64396-273-6
ISBN-13: 978-1-64396-273-3

TABLE OF CONTENTS

Night Windows   3

Bleeders Abound   35

Mouth Bay   57

Vin Scully Eyes   73

White Horse   99

Full Bloom   117

That Dreaded Undertow   127

Rough Tender   141

Tip the Barkeep   157

Not Even a Mouse   173

Angels Live Here   197

For my father, Bruce

Master of tall tales
Conqueror of life

"Ah, Los Angeles!
Dust and fog of your lonely streets,
I am no longer lonely."

—John Fante, *Ask the Dust*

NIGHT WINDOWS

SATURDAY, DUSK

To every detective mulling about the Mansfield Motel parking lot, the twirling berry atop Art Martinez's unmarked might as well have been a propeller cap and he damn well knew it. Maybe he did drop the ball as lead on the last case, but that was for God to judge—although the entire department was doing a fine job of it. Mistakes were common, everyone knew, but he was the last to make a major boo-boo. The pie was on his face. He got the call a good half hour ago. Should've been here in five minutes, the motel not far from his condo. For this, he knew he was walking into fire. He parked the sedan street side, ghetto bird whirring above. Plain cars had their doors open; beat boys stood behind them, guns drawn on a room's window. Looks on the faces of detectives Turnblatt and Marsh were as if he'd walked up to lick their loafers.

Turnblatt: "The fuck were you, Martinez? And don't say church."

"Dinner with the fam. Got here as soon as I—"

Marsh chimed, "What, you eat your meals in the Valley now?"

Martinez brought the dialogue back to work. "What's the status?"

Turnblatt sucked a front tooth. "That couple on the run— pawn shop in some fly-over state. Call came in said they're

3

holed up in Room 9. Heard earlier this week they were probably headed to L.A.—now here we are."

A megaphone barked its usual cop demands.

Turnblatt handed binoculars to Marsh, passing them in front of Martinez. The room's venetian blinds began to shimmy.

Marsh: "He's in there. I'm looking right at him."

Megaphone barked, "COME OUT WITH YOUR HANDS UP!"

Martinez, sensing this was all the info he was going to get off his peers, rushed over to the first patrol car, brandishing his weapon and kneeling before the officer: some kid, barely out high school. The short jog nearly had him winded, stomach gurgling—that poutine a mistake for supper. The kid spewed: one male perp unresponsive, one female deceased near the bed, possible firearm reported by the anonymous caller—tear gas about to be launched to defuse the situation. Martinez crept upwards, noticing a Nissan 370Z with Texas plates parked at Room 9. Something moved inside; the glint off the perp's eyeballs flashed through blind slats.

Well, the fucker's responsive now.

Every cop here knew there were two ways this could go: true north or dead south.

FRIDAY, MIDDAY
(One Day Earlier)

Fuckin' norms...

From a Mexican joint on Olympic, Bess Little gazed upon a nearby carwash pulsing with lunch-hour stiffs, fluffs having their leased cars waxed and dress shoes spat on by some cripple with a shine box. Her beau, Trent, was too busy scarfing his fourth *lengua* taco to notice; she dared not kill his buzz.

Downtown L.A.

She took in the drive-thru business hacks again. *Worse than cockroaches,* she thought. If the world had balls like her man here—nearly choking a mouthful—it'd burn to hell that much faster.

Norms…

Who needs 'em?

She rose from the table to refill an Orange Bang!, catching a glimpse of her shaved head in a mirror blasting Modelo. She looked the way she felt. Two days on the road, nonstop, gunning from a past deed that slimed their boot heels. Every gas stop or liquor store brought questionable eyes. This was the first real meal (outside chips or jerky) they'd had since Las Cruces. The soda fountain belched. A cashier demanded another dollar fifty. Bess splashed quarters before him, just outside his grasp. She admired Trent on the way back, elbows glued to the table, his snout practically moving the foam plate for dregs. This would be the mess hall view if he were incarcerated—same for her if they both got pinched. She put the image out her mind, knowing damn well they were prepared for blowback: *Plan B is now in effect.*

"Should we grab burritos to go, T?"

Trent looked up at her for the first time in minutes. "Nah."

"Time's a wastin'…"

"You said it, Pumpkin. Let's move."

Their photos popped up in a news feed on Bess' cell as they plowed through Tucson. A blonde female in sunglasses accompanied by a square-shouldered male donning a black balaclava and Stetson; Dallas police were on the hunt for two ghosts, both having altered their appearance beyond that night in the pawn shop. Couldn't believe the owner had called the cops—after all, what they took wasn't clean money logged in his books. Then again, Trent's bullet exploded the guy's wife's heart, and that would've drawn an ambulance. T gave them both orders but they acted like a bunch of twits. The bitch deserved what she got—another dummy turned dummy.

There was a string of questionable motels along Washington at the west end of Mid-City. The first one they pulled into was named The Gem and was anything but. They weren't against slumming; however, for Plan B to work, something with a little charm was in order. The Mansfield was a cozy motor inn featuring two adjacent pink buildings the shape of cheap marshmallows. Its ruby neon and location across from a store named Liquorama sealed the deal. They approached a sign beaming *Night Window* in blood red and checked in under Mr. and Mrs. Lamb. The clerk was slovenly, four-eyed and too sucked into one of those judge shows out his mini Zenith to stare back at them. To Bess, the faces inside these night windows were all part of the fun in this life, every strange puss beyond odd and lonesome. They'd witnessed many a poor bastard on the road, another type of norm—ones that threw in the towel the day they were born.

The room lacked pizazz, a scent of its last inhabitant lingering worse than a wet cigar. Bess peeled a long black hair off one of the pillows; Trent dropped their bags and left to park their hot Nissan up the block, away from the motel, until its presence would be necessary.

Bess had removed all the bedding, using a crimson bedsheet to drape over the blinds, creating a sultry atmosphere. She'd changed into a skimpy violet bikini and covered her bald head with one of her many costume wigs—a turquoise one. That long blonde one she used in the stick-up had been tossed by the roadside near Odessa. The lone chair in the room was used to prop a computer; she made sure its camera picked up her entire frame while revealing nothing of her whereabouts. Barbell piercings at her clavicles looked pink enough for antibiotics. She was ready to sign into her live cam account, one she'd set up under the name Trinity in the Small Tits category of a prominent host site, specifically for this occasion. For well over a month now, she'd established frequent visitors, fans really, to come and watch her play. She counted how many roadside inns she'd set up her sex toy show, then lost track. Took a few weeks to find the right guy. She'd created a fake contest for fans to win a date with her, already knowing the lucky bastard. She even stopped conversing over the feed with him; they'd been texting for a bit. She constantly switched out burner phones, remaining a question mark in the life of *her* mark. He lived in Los Angeles, same build as Trent, a tad more brown hair. She sent him a text, letting him know she'd be live in a few. As her chipped nails punched the cell, Trent walked in with two bottles of champagne.

A midnight blue whistle rested in Grady Buchanan's lips, teeth biting down on it every time one of his girls missed a forward pass or drew a yellow card. Soccer practice, Los Angeles High. The matching shirt he had on blasted The Mighty Romans with a profile of their mascot. When first asked, an assistant coaching gig sounded like a shit job. After marinating in the idea, it took hold once his father said it'd look good to superiors, him being an active participant in after-school activities. With a few seasons under his belt, maybe he could parlay this chore into teaching at another school, one near a beach, Redondo or Hermosa. It would also curb the students' judgments of his crude tattoo, a hissing snake under an earlobe, the only one he couldn't cover up; a token from dumb, defiant youth. *Ma and Pop, how I miss them both.*

A voice called from behind him. Monica, a short, stout Mexican who he'd grown soft for. She didn't belong on the team but they were down a few players this year. She asked to use the gym restroom. "Hurry. Sprints start in ten." The girl ran off. He'd slipped up and told her she'd get to start next game, forgetting it was the beginning of playoffs. *Some coach.* She'd understand. He blew the whistle, feeling a vibration from a rear pocket. His phone, a text: *Who wants to see their baby in ten minutes? Private room. You know the drill.*

Grady typed; eyes baked by fever. He blew the whistle, getting the attention of another assistant coach. "Hey Tom, I gotta use the head." Tommy nodded, placing his own whistle between chapped lips, eyeing girls clawing their way to the ball, awaiting fouls.

The main perk of teaching biology here was having his own office tucked in the rear of the classroom. Sure, they stored dead frogs and pigs and cats inside it during dissections, but outside of the dean and principal, a private office didn't exist on campus. He turned on his laptop, locking the office door behind him. Trinity's live feed was stored in his favorites bar—Doris, that was (Trinity was her stage name). Another text pinged as the computer was firing up.

Guess where I am?

Los Angeles?

Bingo. You get a prize.

Her nude image came onto the screen, blue wig nearly the same hue as his shirt. She had large nipples and a thick pussy, one built for a girl twice her size. He sat back, squeezing his cock through sweatpants. She paused from strumming herself, grabbing the phone beside her and punching another text.

So?

What?

Where we gonna meet up?

Wherever you like?

Okay, I'll pick. Come to the Westin.

That rotating lounge. 34th floor.

When? Tonight?

Tomorrow. 1 P.M.

He thought about their playoff game in Carlsbad at noon. He eyed the screen, Doris' fingers back to evil ways. *I'll have to skip it, then.* Not like he was the head coach.

See you then!

The framed four-by-six on his desk of his departed parents

stared back in disgust. He begged forgiveness, then slid down his pants to get primal.

FRIDAY, TEN TO MIDNIGHT

Detective Martinez looped his unmarked through K-Town, over and over, delaying going home to Izzy and the kids, not prepared to break the news that a department transfer could be in the works. His wife would ask why and he'd have to point a fat thumb to his heart. He parked the car on Vermont and strolled toward the beckoning blue haze of the Monte Carlo, a blink of a joint that poured scotch into bowls. He exchanged nods to regulars, cozying up to the murky elbow of the bar. Barkeep slid him a Dewar's; he splashed bills across the counter to keep them coming. Song out the juke felt like a dagger.

So, take a letter, Maria, address it to my wife
Say I won't be coming home, gonna start a new life...

A short Filipina, shimmering in a sequin blouse, came behind him and rubbed his shoulders. He placed a palm on her right hand. "Not tonight, Mona."

"Massage will make you alive."

"I know, dear. But not tonight, alright?"

"Next time."

"Sure, sure."

"What's wrong? Something a matter?"

"Don't get me started." He gulped a hearty pull.

"Can't be that bad. You kill somebody? You police. They deserve it, no?"

"No, I...bungled a case."

"This' L.A. Plenty more cases to work." Mona slid atop the stool beside him.

"Yeah, maybe not for me in Mid-City anymore. They're gonna ream my ass, I know it."

"What you do?"

He thought of poo-pooing her, then got lost in the glitter about her eyebrows. "Evidence led us to a house in Jefferson. Homicide my partner and I were working was of a young girl, teenager—strangled, raped, the works. Anyway, we head to the last address of our main suspect...I dunno, must've heard somethin' from a neighbor's house—a girl in distress. I fuckin' saw red, Mona. Kicked the door in without a warrant."

"She okay?"

"There was no girl inside. Just some dude."

"Your guy?"

"So we thought. Our guy moved out the past month. This was some schmo—an off-duty bus driver who we kicked the shit out of. They got him at Good Samaritan, tubes galore. You'll read it in the papers tomorrow. Took us off the case and suspended my partner, Edgars—a good kid. He took the brunt of the lashing. A solid favor." He slurped scotch. "As of tonight, I'm on ice till word comes down."

"Geez Louise."

"You said it, dear."

He fingered another round for him and Mona. They both sat, staring at their tired reflections in the top shelf mirror, stewing over decisions in both their lives that had brought them to these stools at this bar in this city...at this very moment.

Trent hadn't been back among the lost angels of Santa Monica Boulevard since before his last stretch for armed robbery. After that fall, he figured the city didn't love him anymore and ran east. He met Pumpkin not long after. Downtown Vegas. Fremont Street: another boulevard built on blood. He exited the bus at La Brea, walking toward a lone newspaper stand. He purchased a soft pack of reds and one of those L.A. ball caps with zero team allegiance—ones worn by day laborers and German tourists. The champagne had him buzzed with a taste for something else—something more. He cinched the cap's bill over his eyes, sparking a smoke, heading east toward darkened side streets. His shadow projected a hulking menace. He walked briskly, weary of five-O. There was one objective: executing his part of Plan B.

At the far end of a Walgreens parking lot, he found an eye-raising group of girls. Well, some were girls—and of the pack, only two were white. He hopped a low brick wall bordering the lot and approached them. Three of the girls broke off to smoke something behind a far dumpster. He pointed at one of the white girls, an obvious runaway or silver-spooner turned junkie, down on her luck. The girl sauntered up in powder blue pumps and a sheer dress she wore like a coat hanger. She jabbed to a shadowy corner where they could talk.

He held out smokes. "Wanna grit?"

She took one. The light from his match danced about pockmarks on her cheeks. They puffed away for a spell, both scanning the perimeter for anything suspicious.

"What you want?"

"Half an' half. Plus, a hookup on some Mexi Mud?"

"Black horse? I might know someone."

"He your pimp?"

"*She*'s my friend. Ain't never had no pimp. Who's *your* pimp, brother?"

He grinned, a crooked canine peeking out. "Listen, let's go score, then hit my place—motel up the block."

She put a hand out, nails a toxic orange—same color as the donut hut across the way. Trent eyed her over once more, then peeled off some cash from his roll. Gal was a little too tall, but he'd make it work. She'd do just fine.

"Friends call me T."

She swiped bills from his palm. "Camie."

"Well, Camie...shall we?"

They walked into the neighborhood, razorblade palms blacking out the moon.

* * *

The way she held her smoke, between the ring finger and middle, reminded Trent of Pumpkin. The girl was barely out her teens, her connect for heroin barely out diapers. Least she looked like jailbait, life still revolving around Robert Smith and Morrissey. Camie took him to the girl's tiny studio, some cottage cheese ceiling fiasco at the edge of Boystown. Her name was...well he never got her *name*. Camie called her Raven. Trent peered out the window, eyeing the shuttered Formosa Restaurant, cowering like a beetle under the hellish glow off a Target sign.

"Hey, *Raven*...you ever hang at the Formosa before they closed it?"

Raven gave a *fuck-you-talkin'-bout* stare.

Camie said, "I did. When I first came to town. There wasn't a superstore behind it then."

Trent eyed Camie as if he'd underestimated the girl; her disheveled shell put whatever L.A. cred she had well beneath her years. "A time capsule. I mean, I don't remember it being that great but...to think, right? Cool spot."

Camie finally cracked a smile, hitting her smoke like Pumpkin.

Raven handed over the goods. Black tar. Jalisco.

Trent blew her a kiss as Camie opened the front door.

He texted his sweetheart that they were en route. Earlier, she'd taken the ice bucket and visited that manager with the unhealthy *People's Court* complex. One of the things Trent loved most about Pumpkin was her ability to put all bullshit aside to get what she wanted. A true lady in command of her powers. Her ice bucket endeavor brought keys for the adjacent room overnight, Room 9—on the arm, the manager's pleasure. Didn't have to blow the guy or nothing. Simply talked to him. Pretended to care. The first customer in months. He was a Capricorn. She was rewarded.

Trent guided Camie by the elbow, a taste of chivalry he'd seen in a Bugs Bunny cartoon. They'd already made a pit stop at some dive for a pint, taking turns in the bathroom with tinfoil and a glass straw—the way Camie liked to smoke it. Needless to say, they were both on the nod before scrambling onward.

Camie made herself comfortable, kicking off pumps, calloused toes spreading for relief atop Room 9's coffee table. She lit another of Trent's smokes, clawing her nose in a familiar way. He'd placed a bottle of Wild Turkey on the lone dresser along with two plastic cups before he left to catch the bus. Camie giggled in a flirtatious way; he knew Pumpkin probably had an ear to the wall on her side now. She wasn't the jealous type either, just making sure he was right on track. He handed Camie a cup with a finger of whiskey.

The scent tinged her nostrils; she put it on the table.

"Drink up. Booze'll eat through that cup."

Camie's eyelids bounced at Trent, ready for another taste.

And he had just the taste for her.

Could feel Pumpkin's sinister smile through the goddamn wall. "How 'bout we make a deal?"

"Shoot."

"I give you most the tar I got left. You give me a little bit more than half an' half."

"Bareback? Greek?"

"The latter."

"Throw in another fifty and it's all yours." She slithered out her dress, turning into the sofa, sunning her buns.

He ran a palm across her cellulite rump and then started to undress.

Camie was on the bed now, ass up, awaiting her chore. Trent grabbed a rubber out his wallet, along with a concentrated gob of tar, the heart of his stash—size of a smasher marble. He approached Camie, able to smell hours of walking the boulevard skunking her naughty bits. He opened the condom and spat on her asshole. Before she could finish a fake, "Ooh," he jammed the tar deep inside her with a condom wrapped thumb. When he refrained from completing the deed they'd agreed upon, she asked what he was doing. He went to the bathroom sink, washing his hands while meeting her stare in the mirror. Plan B would begin shortly, her body collapsing, then convulsing—life draining from her in a state of toxic bliss. He pulled a toolbox from out the bathtub, along with a rusty hatchet. Camie's eyes screamed before her body shut down. Trent went for the whiskey and sat at the coffee table, sipping, watching—ready to get to fucking work.

Bess heard the commotion in Room 9 but didn't bother to budge—computer screen locked between her knees on the bed, smoking a joint she stole off some fogey in Austin. The sweet smoke had her in that happy zone, where the weight of the world was held back by a dense wall of cotton balls. Like most things in her life these days, the Facebook page she was using was fake. She set it up in Albuquerque, a day or so after Trent thought he'd swept her off her feet, saving her from double shifts at the Golden Gate, serving drinks to gamblers. *Who in the hell thinks they've rescued anyone from anywhere by taking them to Albuquerque?* At first, she set up the page to snoop— you know, a fly on some *Matrix* wall. Turned out, she never really snooped on anyone but her mother. State of Nevada gave Mother sole custody of Dominic, a child Bess hadn't planned on before (or after) his birth. And that was fine, Mother raising Lil' Dom the same way she'd raised her Bessie: church every Sunday, a rosary for each dirty word. Guilt bred fear in most, but with Dom being *her* son, she knew sin would tickle his funny bone the same way, always begging a scratch.

The computer screen cast a golden glow about her face. Dom was in elementary school, doing well (per Mother's post). *Oh, good for him.* She touched the screen, a picture of Dom in a lavender AYSO uniform. A goalie. *Probably not too coordinated.* She remembered the scent of his first onesies better than any car freshener she'd ever bought. She'd wanted to be a mother...after finding out she was preggo. But that gear never kicked in. Not like the kid could hang with his daddy, either. Could've been any number of fools she'd taken on The Strip—suckers who'd leave their big winnings on the dresser after a pity fuck. A well of guilt rose up her esophagus (first for herself, then for Dom). She clicked out the picture, puffing another plume and snapping the computer shut.

Could hear T in the next room, almost like he was speaking an octave louder so she could partake in the act. Long as the bitch (any white bitch) ended up dead in that room tonight—that's all she cared about. She went over to the closet and removed a bowling bag—their score—the whole enchilada. The sight and feel of roughly three hundred thousand never got old. She'd give Trent a big smooch when it was all over, maybe let him paint her toenails. Big balls and a small brain, the perfect man—how she dug all her chew toys.

SATURDAY, MIDMORNING

The hangover pounding Martinez's temples was nothing close to the tension filling his family's minivan: Izzy speechless to the point of rage, his chubby twin boys (eight years old) carrying on as if he'd been dead for years...*Maybe I had, on the inside?* His glassy eyes met Monica's in the far back seat, his princess, all decked out in soccer gear, excited at the prospect of starting her first JV game. After all, Coach Buchanan had promised. Martinez being temporarily off duty until word came down, he jumped at the chance to drive down to Carlsbad and catch his baby girl kick a ball.

Izzy finally opened her wide mouth to speak as they hit gridlock near Camp Pendleton.

"Artie, we're hungry."

He leered at the woman's jowls, wondering what had happened to the girl he'd married. "We had McDonald's an hour ago."

15

"Monica needs her carbs—she's about to score ten goals."

The boys, Hector and Ivan, shouted their fast food wants. Monica remained silent, butterflies in her stomach now floating around her head.

He smiled at Izzy and was met by a chill. "I know a good California burrito spot in Oceanside. Be there in ten." He wondered what kind of case could've been on his desk by now— a drug deal gone bust, a drive-by with slain civilians? Work was his only solace, a break from this familial cage he'd crafted.

Izzy got back to brooding out the window.

Even if he did get transferred to a new precinct, didn't mean they'd have to move from the condo. His commute could turn to shit, but his pay wouldn't get cut. None of this would impact Izzy. He stewed as an army helicopter flew overhead, blocking out his boys' excitement, contemplating family man miseries.

He was admiring a pair of small birds—black phoebes—canoodling on a tree branch when Izzy shouted something, forcing him back to Earth. "What'ya mean he's not gonna be here?"

Izzy's eyes rolled, yet again. "Coach Buchanan has the flu. Ain't. Gonna. Be. Here. Understand?"

Buchanan, you fucking dunce.

Martinez had met the guy once. Maybe it was the badge shining from his Dockers, but Grady Buchanan had a hard time meeting him eye to eye. And that goddamn tattoo on his neck. What a joke. He'd like to see how Grady fared walking in *his* jurisdiction, gang warfare raging, life as meaningless as this bullshit flu excuse. His detective instincts kicked in, gauging the situation. Monica was now crying in the car, unable to face the fact she wouldn't be starting. Her head coach, Kelley, was by a far goal post, righteous, going over lousy defensive plays with his "A-team."

Who the fuck was he to say my baby girl couldn't play?

Izzy's grating voice: "Well, he is the coach, stoopid."
As options disappeared, red washed behind both eyes. The girl would play. He jumped up from his seat and started down the stands.

Izzy sipped a fountain drink the size of her head. "What are you doing, Artie?"

He swatted the back of a hand to silence her, adjusting his badge along the waistband, making sure the whole world could see it. As he approached the huddle, the badge reflected sunlight, nearly blinding Coach Kelley.

"Need a word coach. *In private.*"

Izzy watched her hubby usher Coach Kelley to the rear of their minivan. She couldn't hear what was being said but could tell by the coach's demeanor that it was a one-sided conversation, a sharp finger stabbing his chest. Sure, Art was often good for nothing more than a paycheck—heck, he never even gave the kids hugs. But this…this was what he did best. What they paid him for: to drill the fear of death into weaker beings.

Martinez caught his breath, opening the minivan's door, having Monica come out to follow her coach onto the field. He climbed back up the stands and sat beside Izzy, a twisted look on her melon. "What?"

"What did you say to him?"

"Ah…nothin' really. He knew it was a great idea, her starting. Just had to remind him why."

She placed a hand on his thigh.

He looked down at it, then back to the field, thinking that now this little road trip had
been worthwhile.

The thought of finding a pay phone in Los Angeles was beginning to hurt Bess' noggin, then she remembered seeing one out front of that carwash, rusty and lonesome, as if it remained only for nostalgia—a pre-millennium relic for folks to point and giggle at.

Trent was asleep when she darted out for donuts and coffee. He was still snoozing when she returned, the long night having depleted him.

The life of a killer on the run.

She made herself up before catching a bus on Olympic into downtown. There'd be over an hour to kill before she was due at the Westin. The attire she wore was very conservative considering her live cam demeanor. With a two-piece suit Mother had loaned her money to buy for a job interview she never had, Chelsea boots and a taut auburn bob, Bess blended with the carwash norms as she wolfed an *asada* taco, dropping coins into the pay phone.

Neither mother nor Dom picked up on her first two attempts. She sipped an Orange Bang!, taking in the atmosphere like a bored chameleon—Benz, Porsche, Rolls—all being detailed by immigrants, underpaid slaves roasted by an angry sun. *This is what it must've been like between knights and serfs in medieval times...*

So much for cultural advancement.

Fuckin' norms, rich or poor, as progressive as this pay phone.

She deposited more coins; three rings and an answer.

"Hello?"

"Mom."

"May I ask who's speaking?"

"Ma, it's me. Put Dom on the—"

"Bessie?"

She wondered about the old coot's mental state. "*Yup.*"

"Oh, this is Jan Kilbourn, a next-door neighbor. Your mother is at the hospital—"

"She okay? What's the deal?"

"Deal?"

"What happened?"

"Oh, it's not her, Bessie. Her grandson, I mean, um..."

"My son!"

"There was an accident. He was on his skateboard and a

motorist either didn't see him in the street or was intoxicated...they really don't quite know—"

"How bad is it?"

"He's stable...but they have him in a coma. Your mother asked for me to listen for the phone in case other family members...or you...were to—"

"What hospital?"

"Sunrise Children's—"

"I'll be there as soon as I can."

Jan began to speak; Bess slammed the phone on its receiver, a tinge of pain rising at her tear ducts before she swallowed it back down.

Is this what all those perfect moms felt?

Is that gear finally kicking in?

She thought of that loot in the closet and her focus returned. Plan B. In a carwash window, she composed herself, reapplying lipstick, checking for salsa droplets. All was well, she a hot little number. She trudged through the ant farm of norms cluttering up Figueroa, wanting to throw elbows but keeping things civilized. She'd make this rendezvous right on schedule, the Westin's tall chrome cylinders shining up ahead.

SATURDAY, NOONISH

Trent rose from his deep slumber, mouth cottony, in dire need of some water or a beer. He scratched his balls and went to the bathroom sink, a note for him waiting on the toilet seat. She'd gotten breakfast, the doll. He ate three long johns, dunking them in weak coffee, beyond lukewarm. He slid into clothes and headed back over to Room 9 for some unfinished business with Camie.

He started in with the hatchet during the early morning hours, but the noise made by the bed's snapping box spring was much louder than he'd anticipated. In fear of rousting any other motel guests (he wasn't sure if there were any), he put the chore aside. There was time. The television was an old cube from the mid-nineties. The picture wasn't crystal but the sound worked fine. He stepped over Camie's frozen corpse, covered with a bedsheet, and flipped the tube to an action flick, some Michael Dudikoff number. He pitched the volume as high as it would go—guns blasting, samurai swords slashing.

Breaking a hole in the box spring didn't take but fifteen minutes, enough time for thirty-plus ninjas to be killed on TV. He braced both legs and straightened his back before lifting the girl. She weighed maybe a hundred but was awkward as hell. *That's one thing movies never show*, he thought. *The blooper reel behind every murder.* Who the hell was going to remove all those dead ninjas anyway? Some poor bastard's thankless job. He dumped Camie into the box spring and kicked the mattress back on top. With the Wild Turkey, he hoisted a toast: *To all them thankless fuckers.* He put what little was left to his lips and turned to watch another ninja explode off a motorcycle.

Grady pulled his PT Cruiser into the Westin's subterranean parking garage, blue flames up its hood bringing a laugh to the valet crew. He rode escalators into the lobby, posters of various films shot on the premises lining the walls: *Blue Thunder, Hard to Kill, Escape from L.A.* Dozens that he'd seen most of. *This could be a nice little conversation starter.* Hadn't been on any dates in well over a year. Sure, there were barroom one-nighters here and there—a local barista turned fuckbuddy. Nothing on the level of what he and Trinity/Doris felt between them. She was special—unlike any girl he'd ever dated. For one, she lived a life less ordinary, which was…almost refreshing when he thought about it. With both parents gone, there'd be no awkward family introduction. This could be a very real thing. That is, if she loved him too.

A glass elevator shot him up thirty-four flights; he watched cars flow across the 110 until its doors opened at the BonaVista

Lounge, a pleasant setting with stunning panoramic views of the Southland—its floor rotating 360 degrees every hour. The hostess took him down to a prime table at a window, having him brace his step as they descended. A sizzling steak appetizer was rushed past by a server, sparking his appetite. The waitress asked if he'd like to order a cocktail while he waited for his guest. He almost blurted, "Bud Light," but caught himself. This was a special occasion. A time to live.

Fuck it.

"I'll have a sloe gin fizz."

Martinez shriveled in his seat, the score now five to zip, his girl not quite the sweeper he'd hoped she was. Izzy's incessant screams had paralyzed Monica, now a spastic mess on the field. Agile athletes on the opposing team dribbled around her as if she were an orange cone, scoring at will. Martinez could feel Coach Kelley lasering him from the sideline; he ignored him, as if all was peachy. At the whistle for halftime, Martinez met Kelley's gaze, nodding once to let coach know that this massacre could be stopped.

Izzy waved gelatinous arms. "Artie, what's he doing?"

Monica exited the huddle, greeted by a water bottle on the bench.

An ice cream truck pulled up in the distance. Without answering his wife, Martinez turned to the boys. "Who wants a banana split?"

Musso & Frank Grill, Hollywood

Trent licked gristle off his fingers before downing his third martini (and sidecar) at the notorious mahogany bar—same one where Bogart and Bacall got frisky. That New York strip was worth sixty dollars. He forgot sides weren't included, hunkering down more cash for sautéed mushrooms and garlic toast.

Pumpkin would be mad at this reckless lunch, but he was a growing boy—needed plenty of energy to pull off this next task. *When will I ever be back in L.A. after today?* This was a celebration.

It was a lame Saturday along Hollywood Boulevard, tourist season all but gone, junk pushers sleeping off the night previous. The terrazzo sidewalks looked much too clean, stars almost twinkling. Someone desecrated Donald Trump's, painting a white hood with eye slits at its crown. *Same town, different year.* He thought of his favorite strip joint (The Cave) and drinking well (Bar Deluxe), now both extinct. Hollywood was always influx, old cannibalized by the new.

The storefront featured lingerie worn by mannequins out a Russ Meyer flick, their tan nipples poking through sheer negligees for every teen to ogle. Trent barged inside, confident, calm. Just a legion of dildoes and rough trade leather, no biggie. What he came for was on a far wall. A curvy brunette with inflatable tits came over.

"Can I help you with something?"

"Need a blonde wig."

"Certain style or cut?"

"Has to be long—not Lady Godiva—'bout the length a your hair."

She smirked, capped teeth leading him to the far wall. "I don't mean to be intrusive but...will this be for you or a lady friend?"

"A woman."

"Okay. That helps with sizing."

"Younger sister—cancer—stage four."

"I'm so sorry."

"Yeah...well."

"Let's get her something special."

Trent licked his lips, eyeing the arch in the girl's back as she reached up the wall, taming the beast that begged to touch. He cracked his neck and stepped back to admire the view.

* * *

Bess didn't bother to remove her large raspberry-framed sunglasses as she scoped the revolving lounge for her mark. A hostess greeted her; Bess stepped around the girl as if she were a bronze statue, taking in the atmosphere. *Tall windows, floor to ceiling— sunlight baking panoramic splendor.* She pushed any thought of her son's incident out the brain and refocused. Her mark was there alright, sitting by his lonesome, gazing out at Chinatown— a clown drink at his fingers. She didn't expect him to notice, but he did. Soon as her toes hit the dining room floor, Grady Buchanan (along with every swinging dick in the joint) turned his head. She sat opposite, not allowing for him to get up and pull back her chair. They stared at each other for a prolonged beat. She could smell his weakness. Grady swallowed. A waitress broke Bess' spell.

"And for you, miss?"

"I'll have a beer."

"What kind? We have—"

"Bring me a bottle of beer, honey. Thanks."

The waitress fled.

Bess removed her sunglasses, meeting Grady eye to eye. "Well, here we are."

"Yes."

That's the best he could say? He was wearing a gaudy flannel shirt, thin beard trimmed to a tee. "You're not a lumberjack, are you?"

"What?"

Yes and What. This guy was a total catch. "I'm only joking."

His shoulders slumped. "Oh. Ha. This place is great, right?"

"That's why I picked it, silly. Now...tell me something I don't know."

"Like what?"

"What types of girls you like to fuck? What makes you cum?"

He choked gin fizz. "I...um."

"Grady, relax. There's nothing to be afraid of. I won't hurt you."

"Okay."

More staring, more silence.

The waitress put a Heineken on the table; Bess grinned till the bitch left.

Grady regrouped, the reality of Doris' presence finally calming his nerves. "Hey, do you know how many movies have been made in this hotel? Let me tell you. A *lot*."

Weak-ass motherfucker. "So, where'd you say you were from again, *Grady*? You're a teacher, right?"

"Well, now that you ask...I'm originally from—"

Fuckin' norms...Bess dove into her beer, trying not to tune out, but knowing she couldn't help herself. This little shindig would be the worst part of Plan B. She smiled and nodded, letting the dude blow his wad. Her hand shot up for the waitress, fingers about to snap; a round of shots was in order, the first of many. She sized up her mark, once again. Soon as the liquor took hold, she'd turn cheetah and pounce.

It took some convincing, but Bess managed to get Grady to drop any notion of getting a room at the Westin since he was too drunk to drive. And he was; she bullied him into imbibing out his comfort zone. She'd run this con before, Downtown Vegas— some jerk mesmerized by the Fremont Street Experience. Told him her name was Morticia, and he actually believed her. There was nothing to it: excuse herself to use the ladies' room, tip the bartender to make her vodka shots with water, sit back and wait for her date to turn into putty. Grady was a lightweight too. Probably one of those kids who counted beers out loud during a kegger. Every time he made an excuse to stop or order food, she'd grab his hand under the table and slide it up her thigh. "Alright, just one more."

With only six shots in him, Grady became a blubbering mess,

bleeding his heart out to her about the sudden loss of both parents. Some crash, up near Big Sur. The way he told her was as if he'd just gotten word that it happened, not "well over a year ago." He described their injuries, those he saw when called to ID their bodies. *Jesus*, Bess thought, her frozen heart given a slight thaw. People were craning in their direction. She passed him a napkin, deflecting her stare out the window to the vast Pacific in the distance. Shushing him kindly, the moment struck her; this could be Dom when he grew up, a parentless loner, looking for love and companionship in sordid places. *That is, if he gets to grow up…*

"I'm sorry. Not usually like this, Doris—but…you're the first person to ask me 'bout myself in a long time an'—"

She could picture Dom in a lousy hospital bed…Mother having to bail after visiting hours. *He'd be there all by himself.* Grady caught himself from sobbing, again. Tears swelled in Bess' eyes, tossing a coin in her gears.

"You okay, Doris?"

She nodded, swiping a single tear with a finger. "The world's pretty fucked up, you know?"

"Luckily, we got each other."

He was touching her hand now, the act bringing her back to the task. She mimed for the check; their waitress scowled.

She walked with Grady, arm-in-arm, steadying him in the elevator (which he thought was hilarious), then down to the valet where she helped slide him into shotgun before grabbing keys to his monstrosity of a vehicle and stiffing the valet. She promised he'd love her place, a quaint bed and breakfast with everything they needed to get "dirty." Once out the garage and onto 2nd Street, she pulled her phone from her purse. Grady was fish-eyed out the window, almost as if he were about to hurl. She texted Trent their whereabouts, making sure he stayed the fuck out of her way.

* * *

Trent was finishing up chores when word came that Pumpkin was coming back to the Mansfield. He tidied up Room 9, making sure the bed was neatly made and that Camie's corpse hadn't begun to reek. A few spurts of perfume and the place was downright fresh. Another bottle of champagne was on ice at the coffee table. He eyed the room, making sure nothing was out of sorts. The thought of his girl seducing some sucker didn't exactly sit right, but it was necessary to get out of this bind unscathed.

He returned to Room 8.

In the closet, he retrieved the bowling bag of cash, a Glock G29 and a Browning Buck Mark. He placed the guns onto the bed, opening the bag and tearing the paper bands off every stack. *Conroy's Curiosities & Pawn Parlor.* How Pumpkin knew they had an ongoing poker game in the store's rear, he hadn't a clue. She must've heard it from some Vegas schlub, needing the world to marvel at his gaming expertise. Regardless, they walked into Conroy's as full-tilt marauders, sending trembling hands in the air, scooping every last dollar out a safe under the counter. Maybe he shouldn't have shot that bitch, then again, maybe she should've shut the fuck up when he told her. *Too late for tears.* He stacked the bands in a pile, re-sorting the cash into rows inside the bag. When he was through, a few tallboys greeted him on ice in the sink. He grabbed one, deciding to clean their weapons, just in case. *That's what I can do while Pumpkin finishes the job.* Another judge program came on the tube. He thought of that sad night manager, then cracked a beer, grabbed the guns and listened for the door to Room 9.

Only the chosen could become such devils.

One thing struck him that he'd almost forgot. He exited the room and ran down the block, grabbing the Z and parking it outside Room 9.

The drive back from Carlsbad was (for the most part) silent—an oldies station filling the void of (what was supposed to be) a tremendous day. In the rearview, Monica's eyes were red and puffy, not a tear left to squeeze. Naturally, Izzy placed the brunt of blame on her husband, never even considering that their daughter sucked balls at soccer. Martinez wondered if his wife had known how bad Monica was this whole time, leading him to believe the girl was something she wasn't. Then again, it's not like he'd ever bothered to ask his daughter—maybe even swing by her practice when he was off duty. Those precious hours were spent at the Monte Carlo, hanging with the boys, cops doing cop shit—mostly telling stories; one thing every policeman was gifted at, embellishing mundane exploits.

To erase the day, Izzy suggested they grab an early dinner at some new joint profiled in the *L.A. Weekly*. If Martinez had known the spot was on the coast of Long Beach, he would've kiboshed the idea and drove straight to Philippe's. This place was one of those houses converted into a restaurant, outside perimeter an open patio. Martinez took one look and thought, *I always wanted to eat on someone's front lawn.* Place wasn't in their budget either, "specializing" in Creole/Cajun food. He humored the thought, having been to New Orleans, the tastes cherished in his brain. Izzy ordered a full slab of pork ribs while the kids ate po' boys filled with Alaskan wild shrimp.

He turned to their waitress, a theater major at CSULB (her declaration), and said, "What's this?"

She leaned over to read; he got a peek of her bra.

"Oh, that's pooh-teen—a Canadian dish. Here we put slow cooked brisket over seasoned garlic fries and top it with bacon-infused cheese curds."

"I thought this was a Cajun joint?"

"We do it all, sir."

"I'll give it a whirl."

"Like to add jalapenos, sriracha—an egg over easy..."

"Sounds like a plan. All the above."

He turned to talk to his family, everyone already sucked into their cell phones. He waved back at the waitress to order a double scotch.

Grady was a giggling fool on sailor's legs outside Room 9. Sun rays fell behind the pink structure, crackling motel neon. Bess fumbled with the key, making sure her mark didn't fall back and smack his skull on parking lot asphalt. Then again, if the door opened and he timbered forward onto stained carpet...well, that was a different story. The door unlatched. Bess shot inside, making sure everything was primed before grabbing her sailor.

Knowing exactly what was inside that box spring, Bess grimaced as Grady plopped onto the bed, trying to get back up, a turtle on his back. He was either too drunk or too stupid to notice anything felt off (probably both). Her plan was to get him to the sofa behind that coffee table; if he passed out there, things would be much easier. He began to snore. She rushed and smacked his face, trying to wake him. As she touched his skin, flashes of Dom burst in her brain. She slapped and slapped, trying to will both Grady and Dom from out their slumbers. It was no use; he was a log.

Like Dom.

Without warning, she began to scream, tears of rage smearing mascara.

Trent crashed in from Room 8, a gun in his hand. "What's wrong, Pumpkin? He hurt you?"

Bess wiped her eyes. "It's nothin', T. Got caught up in *the act.*"

"Thought we discussed getting him to the couch?"

She sighed. "Like I planned for this? Fucker has the liver of an eight-year-old." *Dom flashed again.*

"I can take it from here, babe. Relax." He pulled money bands from out his back pocket and tossed them to the floor.

"Why do you have my Glock, Trent?"

"Heard a raucous...then you cryin'..."

She leered at Grady, his breath shallow, neck tat like a Cracker Jack prize. "Where's the dope?"

"There's enough left to put him down. I'll fix him. Go an' grab your things, put it in his ride. Gimme ten minutes and we're off."

She nodded, exhaustion washing over. *This is all too much.* Finally, this world—legions of night windows—had caught up to her. "I gotta blow my nose." She walked into the bathroom.

Trent braced his knees before hefting Grady onto the loveseat. The plan was to shoot him up with the rest of the tar, grab Camie out the bed and splay them together as "a couple ODs." Least that's what the pigs would think. Soon as they hit San Clemente, Pumpkin would place an anonymous call, securing enough time for them to hit Tijuana. He went to retrieve the last of the heroin, debating doing *Grady* the same way he did Camie—or shoving it down his goddamn throat. First, he had to lift Camie out her coffin.

Bess eyed Trent in the bathroom mirror, sliding off the mattress, picking up the dead girl; the blonde wig he'd bought was ratty, suctioned to the girl's dome like an octopus. She was careful of her actions…slowly grabbing the rusty hatchet from out the bathtub. Soon as T spun and placed the girl on the floor, she rushed into the room, swinging the axe at the back of his skull. The blow rocked him to the floor but failed to penetrate his brain like she'd envisioned.

He staggered to a knee, turning in a daze—shocked at her stance, hatchet high above. "No…no, *Pumpkin.*"

"Quit calling me that!"

"I'm sorry. Please…please…"

Her wig slid off, eyes glazed with mania.

"*No, Morticia!*"

The blade sliced through bone this time, and like cow to bolt pistol, Trent went limp.

Pumpkin. God, she was glad to never hear that again. Trent's noodle thought it up the night they met, after she told him her

29

mother named her Morticia since she was born on Halloween. *All lies, naturally.* Duping men had become stale at that time; a greater itch awaited its scratch. Trent was a decent fellow, even better once she realized he was a felon. Did twelve up in Folsom; she never found out why exactly but knew she could press him into doing very bad things. After loading the money bag and her suitcase into the PT Cruiser, she stuffed Trent's things into the closet of Room 8. Trent's and the hooker's dead bodies looked fake, something out a wax museum's house of horrors. She realized for Plan B to work, T's body would have to be slid into that box spring and covered by the mattress; after all, the cops would be expecting one man and one woman, compatible with pawn shop surveillance and the motel's check-in registry. Sure, they'd smell Trent's rotting shell in a few days, but by then she'd be long gone. She tugged at his leg, the heft of her feat becoming a reality. She was confident it could be done— she'd done it before. When it came to moving lifeless men, it was all in her legs.

She made the bed and fluffed its pillows, then took a final look in both rooms, making sure she didn't leave anything stupid behind like an ID. Grady was still snoring on the couch, a glob of heroin at the coffee table, ready to be lodged inside him. *If I killed him, then what would I gain?* As is, he'd simply be in the wrong place at the right time. *Oh, well.* Not like he knew who she really was. No one did, except Mother and Dominic.

Dom.

She slid on her raspberry sunglasses, piled into the Cruiser and sped up Washington. Vegas was about four hours away. She placed a hand on the bowling bag, caressing the score as if it were an ungrateful cat. She'd wait till San Berdoo, place an emergency call to police, then toss the burner cell out the window.

Don't you worry, Lil' Dom.

Mother is coming.

* * *

SATURDAY, DUSK

Martinez was still huddled behind the door of the squad car; the kid beside him starting to tremble soon as officers approached to fire tear gas into Room 9. He craned up for another view of the room's window, stomach grumbling, forcing him to clench his glutes. The silhouette of the occupant was still there behind blind slats. *He wondered what was going through the guy's mind...gazing out at a sea of berries, officers with guns drawn— helicopter shining its light to let everyone know he was finished.* See, we all make mistakes. *He watched as tear gas flared overhead, a hissing barrel of snakes, then shut his eyes in soft prayer.*

Grady pulled back from the blinds once officers approached with hand cannons. His faculties were fried, head thumping in drunken stupor. Couldn't piece together what the hell was going on; Doris' face at that lounge, the last thing he recalled. He began to shiver, these bodies before him complete strangers, the goriest scene he'd ever witnessed. To think, three minutes ago he was sound asleep and now this. The hell happened? Better yet, what the fuck *is* happening?

Gas cans crashed through the window, spewing poison throughout. He clawed for the door but couldn't see his hand in front of him. Coughing, he slid into a ball, collapsing to the floor: a stillborn fetus.

The megaphone blared. "GO! GO! GO!"

Martinez and the kid rushed toward Room 9. A SWAT crew was there, ramming through the room's door, rushing inside with gas masks. Martinez and the others waited for fumes to dissipate, letting SWAT clear the room. The person they brought out, hog-tied in zip-ties, cried like a little bitch. They threw him in the rear of a police cruiser and sped back into the room. Martinez placed his gun in its holster, adjusted the badge on his belt,

peering inside the car. At first, he didn't connect the dots.
Then: that goddamn tattoo!
He nearly shit.
The captive hollered, "Mister Martinez. You gotta help me. I
didn't do this!"
"Thought you had the flu?"
"Listen—"
"And it's Detective Martinez, Buchanan. Get it straight."
"I'm sorry, Detective. But you need to—"
"There's nothing I can do for you, 'cept haul your ass to the
station. Try and bleed my heart down there, son."
"Wait—"
Martinez stormed off, screams out that cruiser like free jazz
to his ears. He raised up on Turnblatt and Marsh, busy taking
notes on Room 9.
Marsh: "The fuck is it now, Martinez? I'm only letting you
hang around 'cause I got lead. Don't need you fucking up my
crime scene, got it?"
"I know the perp—"
"That so?" Turnblatt pointed to the body, "Her too?"
"Nah, only him...personally."
Marsh clicked his pen. "Well then...who the fuck is he?"
Martinez smiled, a shift in power at hand. "Wouldn't you like
to know?" He looked past them at the frozen girl. "You guys tidy
up here. I'll take my guy down to the station and press him."
Marsh: "He's bullshittin'. Look at him—trying to climb out
his own grave."
"Name's Grady Buchanan. My daughter's soccer coach at
L.A. High. See you in a few, cocksuckers."
Before they could fume, his back was to them, perma-grin
washing the previous night's mistakes from memory.
Nine lives.
Six to go?
Damn, it felt good landing on one's feet.

* * *

SATURDAY, 10:08 P.M.

A stretch Hummer roared its way up into the Cajon Pass, the cab filled with six toasted tech boys, en route to Vegas for "Colin's birthday, man." The driver was dead-eyed on the road as hoots and hollers bled from the cab, loud enough to pierce a raised partition. He removed his cap, tossing it to the passenger's seat, contemplating new lines of work. Headlights flashed upon a steaming vehicle, catawampus on the shoulder. The irony of blue flames across its smoking hood brought about the night's first smile.

Twenty minutes up the road, the headlamps cast upon a woman, nicely dressed, towing baggage through dirt and tumbleweed. The driver immediately placed her as the driver of that vehicle, the thought of stopping never crossing his mind—that was, until the partition came down, and one of the techies shouted, "Pull over, bro."

Bess would've waited to place the call to police if she'd known Grady's Hot Wheel couldn't make it up the Cajon Pass. Here she was, sans car, phoneless, walking uphill to find a rest stop or gas station—anything that might help her continue on home. A rustling of broken glass on asphalt came up behind her. She stopped, turning into high beams, then averting back, hand on her Glock inside the bowling bag. The limo's rear door opened. A slender white kid in chinos and topsiders came to ask if she needed a ride.

"Vegas?"

"Yeah—our bro, Colin—it's his birthday and..."

"Sure it's not too much trouble?"

"Our pleasure. We got booze, coke...you name it. Come aboard."

Bess gave a sly grin, brushing past the boy, hugging her cash. He ran to grab her luggage. One glance inside the cab and the eyes on five others nearly exploded out their skulls. The stench of weakness was strong. "Got room for one more?"

The boys clashed skulls, hustling to make room.

"How old you fellas anyway?"

"Old enough," said the one in braces.

Nineties babies.

Kid from outside loaded her suitcase in the trunk and came inside, saying, "Driver, we're ready."

The partition climbed.

Bess refrained from resting her head against the leather, meeting every boy in the eye that introduced themselves.

She was handed a warm beer.

A fat kid lit a joint.

Braces asked, "We never got your name, honey?"

Honey? "Call me Rae."

He slid closer to her, bile on his breath. "Rae...what?"

"Rae Dawn Chong...*honey*. Now, pass me some fuckin' coke."

The limo sped through desert and the party continued. Bess took slugs up her nose. Moonlight pierced the sunroof, another night window; she caught a falling star and made a wish for Dom—a small prayer, one she knew would never get answered.

BLEEDERS ABOUND

I.

He retched on all fours in the alleyway like a dog heaving a bit of T-bone, eyes watering, blood and saliva pooling from his lip onto a torn pizza box, home to a half-eaten breadstick. The occasional car would jet past, illuminating the blackened silhouettes of his aggressors. Bagmen. One shorty, the other a has-been left tackle gripping a crowbar. To think they wouldn't find him was all thanks to the Bushmills. Christ. He should have made for Reno, started fresh. A bookie that ignores the spread on swindling should get out of the game altogether. A final dry heave brought up the two molars. He spat them at the breadstick and rose weary, not quite ready for another much-deserved slug.

The shorty grabbed him by the collar. "Marcus is giving you till morning to ante up—if it were me, I'd say two thumbs and we call it a day. Grab the cash then head to church—you lucked out, Buck-o. Don't make us come find you."

Buck watched the two head out toward their sedan on 8th. His tongue slimed the vacant slots on his gums before hocking another red loog onto the trash bin. The cell beamed ten past ten as he scrolled for that foreboding number. The emergency out—Shizez. Only shark in town he hadn't gone to bed with and for good reason. Now, he figured, *What the hell? You can only die once.*

* * *

Cal's back began to flare as he gently lowered little Carly into her pink Barbie bed, shaped like a mini-Corvette. She was tuckered out from their long day at Venice Beach, pointing at weirdness and filling up on funnel cake for dinner. Her porcelain nose twitched the moment her head hit the pillow. Stroking her blonde curls filled his belly with regret. Nearly four and still calling her step-dad Pop. That was all on him, but not anymore. Belinda was letting him back into their world, one weekend a month. He wasn't about to screw up twice.

Belinda walked with him outside, one of the more cordial moments they'd shared in years. She still wore that awful vanilla drugstore perfume. He opened the door to his taxicab, a snot green Crown Vic, the top light beaming.

"You're growing on her, Cal. You know that?"

He smiled, strumming his sallow beard. "Hope so."

"Gonna be there tomorrow? Her dance troop goes on at ten."

The thought of scantily clad little girls gyrating to Madonna was ridiculous to him, but Belinda's stern look had him bite his tongue. "Sure thing."

"It's at Pershing Square. Don't be late."

He pulled the cab from out the driveway, noticing Belinda's hubby glancing out the kitchen window. Fat prick. Cal took comfort in the fact that Carly looked just like him, making that step-fuck see his face every day.

The first dispatch came as he passed Washington on Lincoln, making it back to the 10 east. It wasn't really a dispatch call, just a pilfered feed from the scanner he'd set up to milk other cab frequencies. Being a cabby in Los Angeles was hard enough, but a gypsy cab, now that required cunning—cunning and a pistol. He punched the gas and swerved around a minivan, its rear window bragging of zero birth control with six stick figures.

* * *

The awkwardness of being sandwiched by hairy lugs in the back of a stretch limo was tolerable; the music was what could put a drill through Buck's head. Shizez was a huge Sting fan—not The Police Sting either, the one that fucked up *Dune* and everything thereafter. By the looks of it, the three skirts sliding over him like snakes on an egg were digging it too. Buck sat patient, knowing better than to interrupt an opus like "Desert Rose." He'd heard about this guy—Georgie Mund—sat in the same seat as he was now—who couldn't stop crying during "Brand New Day." Shizez took offense. Didn't matter that he'd just turned Georgie's wife out for not owning up on a two-bill soccer bet, he took his eyeball anyway. Buck just sat, twiddling his thumbs, lucky to still have them, waiting for the ditty to drown out.

Shizez pulled out a small white vile, and the raven-haired beauty removed her top. Buck stared on, wondering how cosmetic enhancements nowadays could leave such dimples. After four bumps off her oval browns, Shizez cut the music with a remote, eyes now black buttons beaming at Buck. The awkward stare had Buck sweaty, focusing on broken marquees whizzing through the peripheral.

"How much?"

Buck adjusted, leaning forward to lessen the squeeze. "Ten grand'll do."

Shizez nodded to lug #1. He slid a briefcase from under his seat. It contained two hundred K, easy. The lug tossed one of the bands to Shizez. The girls grew restless, petting at each other as Shizez peeped on. He fanned the bills over their bodies, sharing his grey tongue with each, accordingly. The band landed on Buck's lap. Shizez pressed a button on the center console. The limo stopped dead in the middle of Broadway. Car horns wailed.

"One day," said Shizez. "The vig is double."

"Twenty?"

Shizez nodded, fiddling with the console again, opening up the sunroof. He nodded to lug #2. "Your brother paid all his debts, that's why I'm being so kind. Be more like him, Buck-o.

Smart."

Before Buck could get the band snug in his front pocket, he was being launched upwards into the night.

The walk up 8th to Fig was quite soothing, a gentle breeze rushing the avenue, chilling Buck's fat lip and swollen jawbone the size of a ping-pong ball. The street was virtually empty thanks to flatfoots in blue polos, ensuring downtown remained sedate. No more fun for anyone, not in the heart of the city. All the favorite spots for loitering and pushing were now on the eastern fringe but who seriously wanted to walk there? A triangle of glass crashed in the street, sending upward glares from the coppers. A window from the Commercial Exchange building had been smashed by squatters, brawling for sanctuary. The cops rushed in, guns high. Buck kept moving.

The Back Door Pub was in an alley just past Flower. The name said it all, harboring only a select local bunch who dared to stumble upon it. Buck was headed there earlier when he ran into the wall of Marcus' goons. He was meeting a friend to make bad on a bet.

The place was quiet; couple patrons trapped in a chess match. The thick barmaid sipped Fleischmann's from the bottle while loading up the jukebox. Buck asked her, "Morty 'round?"

Her eyes swam laps. "Think he's in the shitter."

What a gem.

Buck marched behind the bar for a tumbler, filled it with Bushmills and plopped on a stool. He was three gulps deep, barely feeling his face, when a warm hand cupped his shoulder.

"Thought you were a no show, Buck-o."

"Heya Morty, got the cash." Buck fingered five bills and slid them into Morty's breast pocket.

"The number four came through, buddy boy. I told you—ten to one. You place anything on Starlight Surprise?"

Buck shook his head, wishing he could tell the duffer the

truth. He'd taken Morty's social security moolah and placed it on the nine horse which didn't even break. With new cash fronted, he figured he'd make good with everyone he'd been goading along. He killed the drink. "You know if Tommy's at the Bounty tonight?"

"Yup, just called here with a tip on the first race at Del Mar. You want in?"

Buck smiled. "Nah, ain't feelin' lucky—see ya 'round, Mort."

A reversal of fortune was exactly what he needed, but by the time that race hit tomorrow, it would be too late. He needed cash by morning or he'd be running his own race. Just then, the barmaid goosed him, taunting to share a dance to some Morrissey. He kissed her on the cheek. "Next time, Nikki. I promise." Exiting the pub, he lit a Camel and dialed a cab.

A mound of fresh Kodiak biting the gums was all Cal needed to keep him buzzing through the city till dawn. The hipster couple he'd picked up from The Kibitz Room was headed downtown to The Standard, pickled out of their gourds, not realizing that his meter jumped two dollars every ten seconds. They began necking, so he bumped the fare to forty-five bucks. He spewed a wad of dip gravy into a Big Gulp. A call came in, requesting a taxi at 8th and Fig. He sped up down Wilshire, smashing the two lovebirds apart, back into torn seat cushions.

The hipsters got hip, forcing him to pull over three blocks short. He still got them for sixty-five, sans tip. They barely poured out before he launched back toward 8th.

A white man sat smoking out front of Roy's Restaurant, looked like he'd picked a fight with the wrong wrestler. The brakes squealed as he sidled up the curb. He spat out the window. "Where to, guy?"

Buck looked at the slime-colored heap and got skeptical. "You the taxi I called?"

Cal gave a brown-tooth grin. "Sure—come on in."

One thing Buck could sniff out was a fellow miscreant and this cabbie was one minty bastard. "Before I tell you where to go, you gotta kill that meter."

"Can't do it, friend."

"Listen, I know the score, gyp-gyp. I'll pay you enough to cover the night—" He flashed some bills. "—Just take me to a few spots 'round town. That's it. Shouldn't take but a coupla hours."

Cal racked the prospect of getting in early, having time to wash up and nap before Carly's big dance-off. "Money up front?"

"Half." Buck floated him a hundo.

"You got it—name's Cal."

"Buck—know where the HMS Bounty is?"

"Of course."

"Mind if I smoke?"

"Hey, it's your funeral."

II.

The HMS Bounty was located at the first floor of the Gaylord Apartments in the core of the Wilshire corridor. It used to sit across from the Ambassador Hotel, adjacent to the Brown Derby. Nowadays, those landmarks had been swapped for a Korean strip court and a dirt lot. *Blasphemy!*

Cal pulled into a metered slot out front. They both exited.

Buck asked, "What'ya think you're doing?"

"Going inside, grabbing a beer. You don't look like you're in any shape to take on trouble yourself."

"Trouble?"

"It's written all over your face there. I know *your* kind."

"Really?"

"Don't worry. I'm always game for roughhousing, plus, I gotta make sure the rest of this fare slides in the wallet."

Buck shrugged. "Fuck it. Come on, then."

With hooked fingers, Cal hucked the dip out his jaw and splat it in the gutter. "Incidentals are covered whenever I'm forced off the meter, you know?" He mimed tipping a beer.

"Great. Do me a solid, though. Take off that vest and bandana. What are you, some kind of Willie Nelson renegade?"

"That's good, coming from a man in a purple shirt—your suit looks empty, by the way."

They approached the wood door.

"It's lavender, asshole—Italian."

The Bounty was docile for a Saturday, the inner decorum Hemingway-esque. A few nautical compasses, porthole mirrors and paintings of black sails made it fit for salty dogs. They grabbed a seat at the bar. Buck ordered the usual and pointed at Cal.

"Coors and a shot of whatever he's having."

The tiny Korean bartender said, "Booshmeal?"

"Indeed."

Buck turned from the stool to case the place for Tommy. Nothing but a pack of seniors huddled around the Dodger game replay in the corner. As Cal reached for his beer, Buck saw the blurred tattoo over his thumb—crossbones under a rat skull. He was taken aback. Cal noticed.

"What?"

Buck pulled down his collar, revealing the same brand at the base of his neck. Beneath it, the words *Loyal to None* swung in cursive.

Cal said, "What's your full name?"

"Buck Van Patton."

"No shit? So, you're Bobby's kid brother?"

Buck smiled.

Cal took it in, cautious to respond. "How is Bobby nowadays?"

"Good—outta prison. Livin' in a trailer out past Albuquerque—fixin' toilets."

"Shit, that's better than busting up liquor stores like we used to. Still being a hardass to ya?"

"You know it." He slugged down scotch. "You always go by Cal? Doesn't register."

"The boys used to call me Mongrel."

"*Oh*—you were with Dook when he shot at those Eastsiders on Abbott Kinney?"

"Yeah—Dookie saved my ass that night."

"Really?"

Cal turned away.

It was hard for Buck to fathom the same guy who ate dogshit for dollars as being a hero. Dookie was a dimwit, got his ass killed in Corcoran over a bag of Doritos. "You ever get back to the neighborhood?"

"I drive through occasionally. Got an ex by there."

Buck sat astounded, hoisting his beer. "To glory days."

Cal reciprocated, "Dogtown."

Before the bottles could clank, Buck caught a flash out the corner of his eye. *Tommy.* He was lunging toward him, a flying right cross headed straight for his temple. Ducking, it grazed him but kept on for Cal. The fist thwacked him square on the nose, sounded like a snap of stale celery. Buck got Tommy into a full nelson. Cal's nose began to leak, prompting the barmaid to hand him the counter cloth. He contained the rage.

Tommy squirmed in frustration, "You filthy sonofabitch."

"Easy, Tom, I got your winnings—relax."

Tommy stopped struggling so Buck let him go. He was in good shape for his age. By the looks of Cal's nose, he still had that KO power that floored Baby Bo Bradbury in '72. A true slugger till death. Buck handed him five bills.

Tommy patted Cal, "Sorry 'bout that, champ." He thumbed at Buck. "This Nancy's a greasy one. Lemme make nice." Before he could gesture, the barmaid slid down a bottle. "As for you," he turned to Buck, "we're good but we're through—and if you don't mind, I'll be sitting over there," pointing to the adjacent dining room filled with ruddy puffed booths.

Cal sat, sponging his head, the rag reeking of mildew. He tossed it to the counter, revealing a snout now bowed a bit to the left. "The hell was that about? You a slouch bookie?"

"Kinda. Been placing bets for a few guys 'round town—ponies, baseball, what have you? If they win, some of the time—*not all the time*—I'll come back with their wager and say I couldn't place it beforehand—pocket the winnings." He gauged Cal's pointed brow. "Don't give me shit, man. You drive a gold-bricked cab—what's the difference?"

"I didn't say anything—nothin' at all."

A *last call* holler greeted them inside The Snake Pit on Melrose. The joint was jam-packed, filled with gutter punks out from a show at The Gig. They waded through the sea of studs, patches, boots and bald heads. Place could use a Febreze. The bartender was pouring a PBR in front of a wall of liquor, clear to the ceiling. Buck caught his attention and pointed to the restrooms at the rear. The bartender slid the pint and headed over.

The noise had simmered once back by the pisser. The bartender stood, wiping his hands with a towel, glaring back at them with disinterested eyes.

Buck said, "How you been, Red?"

"Poor."

"Oh yeah?" He pulled out five bills and handed them over.

Red's demeanor persisted, pointing to Cal. "This your boyfriend?"

Buck laughed. "Give us some space, Cal."

Cal backed up a few and turned toward the dispersing crowd. "What's it now, Buck-o?"

"I gotta find some action tonight, something I can turn eight grand into forty—hear anything?"

"Can't help you. The big boys ain't playin' poker tonight—even still, you ain't welcome."

"Any fights going on at the docks later?"

"No—I gotta get back to work." Red turned to leave.

Buck grabbed his arm. "Listen, I'm in deep tonight—owe twenty-twenty to Marcus *and* Shizez. Gotta have it by morning."

"Shit, man. The fuck's wrong with you—Shizez?" Red paused.

"Look at my fuckin' face—*and* Marcus."

"Bobby know about this?"

Buck shrugged in response.

"Okay, but just this once. I got a guy. Lemme see what he says. Hang out a few."

Buck nudged Cal. "Come have a smoke." They walked through the kitchen, into the alley.

Cal waved his palm at Buck's cig offering. Buck lit up and took a hefty pull, staring off in the distance. "Heard all that?"

"Uh-huh."

Buck shoved two bills at Cal. "Little extra for the nose job. Should probably distance yourself from me. Bad mojo."

Cal took the cash. "No worries—never had good mojo, anyways."

The back door opened as Buck let out a jet stream of smoke. Red approached, nodding his head, holding out a scrap of paper to Buck.

"It's a juiced greyhound named Harlequin—running the third at eight to one. Should put you over if he sprints."

Buck shrugged. "Can't wait around till tomorrow, man."

"Track's in Macau."

"China?"

"Night race. Posts at seven ten—their time."

Buck checked his cell. Two twenty. "How far ahead is China?"

"Fifteen hours."

Cal said, "So, it's just after five p.m."

"Hop Louie's your best bet for lying down," said Red. "They always have action on this track."

Buck flicked the cig, grinning. "Red, you magnificent bastard."

"Thank me later, if you don't end up in a ditch. Dan Cannon went three deep with Shizez and nobody's seen him since

Christmas. Be careful."

The cab sat idling at Wilshire and Alvarado. The MacArthur Park spring launched in the rearview, sending ripples along the moonlit pond. Buck was up front, riding shotgun. The drag was a ghost town. They both stared at the giant *Stand and Deliver* mural, hovering above a slew of 99-cent stores and check cashing terminals.

Buck said, "Shit, I remember when I could come down here and raise my rent on a Monday night, just by trolling the dives. Now look at it—it's like an A-Bomb vaporizes everyone at midnight."

The light turned green.

"All the bad shit's still here," Cal said. "You just gotta dig a little deeper to find it." He shifted gears. "Old neighborhood aside, you ever think about why you do what you do?"

"Survival, what else? *You gotta bleed to feed.*"

"What's that?"

"Something my old man used to say, teaching me and Bobby the grift. *Move to a city, bleed everyone you can for as long as you can. When the wells dry up, bail.*"

"Sounds like a shit existence."

"Funny, that's what I used to think. Now look at me—a chip off the ole block." He sparked a smoke. "Least Bobby went straight after prison. Why *you* do it?"

"Been thinking a lot about that lately. Just got permission to visit my kid again—restraining order dropped by the ex."

"How old?"

"Be four in five weeks—a girl—Carly. Now, if you'd asked me why I do this last week, I probably would have said sheer boredom. Never been able to hold down a steady job and I ain't one to lift a shovel. This' easy money and it don't cost much for me to live."

"What about today?"

"Necessity. I can see a future now, with Carly—she called me daddy today, first time. Just not sure how to provide it for her, you know? Not like I can pick up something that pays better at my age. You got kids?"

"Two—twins. Almost in their teens."

"They in town?"

"Nah, Wichita—no, Williamsburg—one of the two. Haven't seen them since they were about your daughter's age. My way of giving them that future you're searching for."

They sat quiet, marinating. Cal gunned the Vic toward Chinatown.

III.

An arch of golden dragons welcomed them into the exotic perils of L.A.'s orient. Streamers and banners heralded the year of the Tiger as they glided up Broadway. Every store and restaurant was closed for blocks. Hop Louie sat at the rear of Old Chinatown Plaza, a mini city of jade accents and red tile roofs, stretching upwards to the stars. Hop functioned as a restaurant by day, nestled at a second floor with a barroom tucked below. The success of its after-hour activities was attributed to appearing closed to the novice eye. Expert degenerates knew better.

Cal reached over and opened the glove box. A Ruger Vaquero fell on Buck's lap. Cal grabbed it and plugged the sucker in a holster up under his vest. "You mind? I'll leave it here, if you know what we're about to get into."

Buck shook his head. "Be my guest."

They marched through the plaza, eyes darting to ensure safety. Buck rapped on Hop's front door several times before fanning a bill at the peephole for a response. The door's innards began to slide and clank. Cal crossed his arms, right hand gripping the pistol as they marched inside.

The barroom was alive, the majority of patrons trapped in

pai gow or card games. A potent Rastafarian sat in front of a single flat screen, projecting results from the first race in Macau. Red Chinese lettering cluttered around a photo finish. The Rasta tore up his ticket, sending it fluttering above his crusted dreads, returning to a snifter of cognac.

Buck and Cal approached the bar, a section of its far wall covered with random napkin doodles of questionable characters. The chiseled bartender nodded from behind a racing form. Buck spoke slowly, hoisting three fingers, "You taking bets...for the third race?"

The bartender sat disillusioned. Buck slowed the question a bit more, attempting to break the language barrier. The bartender approached, placing his hands flat on the counter. "I can understand you, *motherfucker*—and yes, we're taking bets on the third."

The Rasta took notice, approaching. "The fuck's the matter with you, dog?"

Cal couldn't help but chuckle as Buck slank on his stool.

The bartender tossed the racing form their way. Inside were the opening lines on each race, both in English and Chinese. Buck found his winner in the one slot, Harlequin, eight to one.

"Lemme throw down eight K on the third—number one to win."

The bartender swiped Buck's bills from the counter, undaunted by the sum. He counted them below a corner security camera before depositing them in the register. Buck was handed a receipt with his bet info. Cal sat looming the stats on the second race about to post. Buck ordered Tsingtaos.

Cal asked the Rasta, "Who you like in the second, buddy?"

"The four—Tomboy. Won a bit off him a few weeks back."

Cal pulled the three hundred from out his wallet and turned to Buck. "My nose got cracked by a Tommy tonight—you think that's a sign?"

"I dunno. Superstition ain't my bag. What's he at?"

"Sixteen to one." Cal reflected a beat. "Fuck it, sounds like a winner."

The Rasta nodded reassuringly. "If you ain't livin', you're dyin'."

Buck swilled his beer, unsold, trying to drown the night's butterflies.

Cal turned to the bartender. "Let me get three hundo on number four."

The Rasta followed. "Throw me down for fiddy."

The bartender brought back their receipts as they turned to watch the gates break on the screen. With a buzz, the gates parted. A hare lure zoomed at the inner railing, storming out the hounds. Them boys were quick. Tomboy kept pace mid-pack, a smoke-colored beast whose stride could skip across water. Cal stood at the turn and started to yell at the screen.

"Let's go, Tomboy. Come on, Tommy!"

The card and tile players didn't much appreciate this, but he could give a shit. The Rasta joined in just round the turn as Tomboy started to break. "Here we go, Tommy! Move it, boy, move it!"

Buck turned to see for himself. He couldn't believe it. The pooch was gaining.

Cal yelled, "He's gonna take it!"

It was neck and neck for twenty yards before Tomboy pulled away in a trail of dust. Cal yipped, high fiving the Rasta, both of them grinning to high hell.

Buck did the math in his head. He could have pocketed $128,000. Fuck.

Cal and the Rasta exchanged names. He was Homer, the gap in his front teeth still beaming.

The bartender opened the door to a back room behind the bar. Buck could see three guys huddled around a pyramid of cash, each counting stacks with big guns resting beside them. The bartender returned with Cal's winnings, forty-eight hundred. Homer bagged a cool eight. Buck congratulated them both and got back to his beer, anxiously awaiting his dance, posting in twenty.

* * *

Buck was down taking a leak when that triumphant buzz suckered Cal back into the racing form. Homer knew better, leaving with his winnings the moment they'd touched his palm. Buck's juicer had first gate, making him even more desirable. He racked around the concept of letting it ride, until the name of the number six caught his eye—Curly Cue. The hound was an unknown, flown in from Australia. The name ricocheted through his brain. Curly—Carly. Carly had blonde *curly* hair? The line was at twenty to one since the pooch was a first timer in Macau. His palms got itchy. Buck sat back beside him, noticing the form.

"You 'bout to press your luck on my boy, or what?"

"Possible, possible."

The television began to profile each of the hounds now taking the track. Buck's number one looked mean, mouth frothing inside the muzzle, back legs meaty and veiny as a monster cock. The pooch was definitely juiced but Cal wondered just how much he'd been starved.

The number six trotted out, all spotted and scrawny. Cal figured looks could be deceiving since Curly Cue weighed in five pounds less than all the other hounds. *Less weight, more speed?*

Buck ordered a shot of Jäger, rubbing his ticket like a rabbit's foot. He could see it was a lock but it couldn't be over quick enough. The black syrup slugged down his gullet. "I gotta piss."

"Again?"

"I piss when I'm nervous, man."

Buck ran to the head.

Cal gave a *Psssst* to the bartender, thumbing three K.

Buck's hips swayed gently, sending the golden stream clockwise on a urinal cake with a portrait of Mayor Villaraigosa. His cell buzzed his front pocket. "Shit." He wiggled with purpose before stuffing the beast back and reading the screen. *Bobby?*

"Hey, bro. What's up?"

"Nothin', man. Just checkin' in."

"How's Albu-crappy?"

"Better than a steel cage, sometimes. Heard you're in a tight spot."

"What? Nah."

"Twenty-twenty? Fuckin' *Shizez*."

"Red told you?"

"Had to call me in the middle of the fuckin' night too."

Buck rubbed at the Harlequin ticket. "I'll be alright."

"You know I hate worryin' about your dumb ass."

Buck deflected. "You're not gonna believe who I'm having beers with right now."

"Who?"

"Mongrel!" He laughed before noticing the silence on the other end, further clarifying, "From the neighborhood."

"Cal Pappas?"

"Yeah!"

"The fuck's the matter with you, boy. That fucker got Dookie sixteen years in Corcoran."

"Huh? I thought Dook saved his ass that night on Abbott Kin—"

"You thought wrong, motherfucker. He's the one shot at those kids. Knocked out Dook and put the gun down his pants—left him there, fresh meat for the po-po's."

Buck's gut dropped, confused. "I-I didn't know."

"Why would you? Maybe if you'da come visit me in the clink *once*, I woulda told you 'bout it. Too busy knuckles deep in your own shit, like always."

"I'm sorry, man. I—"

"Wherever you at, get the fuck out. That two-bit punk can't be trusted, man. If it wasn't for *embracing* Jesus, I'd go there and put him down myself. Tell him that too."

Buck rubbed the ticket some more. "Okay, Bobby."

Bobby beat him to the hang-up without even a goodbye.

IV.

The gates had barely split and Harlequin led by a length. Another three seconds and it was two. Buck sat back in a moment's relief, shooting look-daggers at Cal. Cal gritted his teeth, glued on number six, trailing dead last. Harlequin pulled four lengths, fixated on the lure, his insides turning at the chance at fresh meat. The hound wasn't just sprinting, he was stalking. Five lengths—six. At the turn, it happened. Harlequin leaped at the rabbit with all his manufactured might. Buck gasped. The pooch crashed into the railing, falling back first to the track, smashing into the pack like a dumbbell on a house of cards. The squeal from the number three and four was heartbreaking. The two and five barrel rolled before limping aimlessly. The number six was resilient, hopping through the heard mid-stride, gunning around the turn, his nimble body shaking by its lonesome on its hot path to glory.

Cal stood but didn't cheer. He didn't have to. The bastard just took it, making him sixty thousand richer. Buck hyperventilated into the bar, anticipating cold tears as Harlequin's trainers tried capturing the beast, now sprinting back toward the gate on the TV behind. It was official; he was a grease spot.

Buck was staring blankly at the counter when the bartender fetched Cal's winnings. The thud of sixty thousand on the bar didn't even jar him. His brain hurt. Cal stuffed the cash into his vest. "Let's go, Buck."

The drive down Grand was silent, Disney Music Hall reflecting the first rays of sunshine off its jagged turd shape. Buck peered out the window, replaying the night's tragic events, getting more furious with every glance at Cal. Fuckin' fink. He thought about that letter he wanted to send Bobby during his stretch but was too afraid his spelling made it unreadable. Should have sent it anyway, taken a bit more abuse to support his only brother.

Cal packed a fresh mound of Kodiak and pulled the cab over at The Biltmore Hotel. He couldn't ignore Buck's broken demeanor. If the kid wasn't Bobby's brother, he would have never thought to offer. Guilt strummed his esophagus. He was a dumb kid that night with Dook on Abbot Kinney. All these years later and he still felt horrible about it, even lying to Buck back at the Bounty churned his guts. It was time to make right with karma, or at least try.

"How much you need, again?"

Buck opened the door. "Doesn't matter."

Cal pulled four stacks from out his vest and tossed them over. "That's forty."

Buck's eyes did a Rat Fink number, the gesture leaving him confused.

"Why—"

"I ain't giving it to you, Buck. It's an investment."

"How so?"

"I'm lookin' to expand the business, grab another cab—bleed this city dry. That forty'll pay itself back as you work. Interested in a new racket?"

Buck took a beat. "When would I start?"

"Immediately—first thing after you make good with those sharks." He got out the cab, signaling Buck to come around and drive. "Take it for the day and meet me here for dinner. Gonna grab a room and crash for a few—got Carly's ten o'clock dance recital at Pershing Square."

Buck got in, Bobby's harsh words echoing inside his dome like an empty walnut.

Cal closed the door and handed him the pistol. "Toss this back in the glove box. Ain't safe drivin' a gypsy in L.A." He headed for the hotel entrance.

Buck gripped the pistol; his palm began to sweat. It could be this easy. He fingered the trigger. "Hey, Mongrel."

Cal turned. Buck stammered words with a look of constipation.

"What's it, Buck-o?"

The generous gesture hadn't had him conflicted. Retribution was warranted for Cal's sin but so was getting the green to Marcus and Shizez. Had to be smart, save his own ass first. Like he had the guts anyway. "Uh...Tommy's got a lead on the first race at Del Mar, you know?"

Cal laughed and kept on. "Fuck off, gyp-gyp."

The brain was on overload. Buck stood under a clocktower speckled with tiled mosaic at Grand Hope Park. Marcus' goons were on their way. He waited, staring at the playground filled with early worm parents and their ugly toddlers. Seniors and homeless were huddled on wood benches throughout. Potential witnesses. That's why he picked the place for the drop, to guarantee his face didn't lose any more pearly whites, hopefully.

The shorty showed up on time, noshing a Chicago dog, sidled by a different heavy, more the linebacker type. Buck handed the dough to the linebacker, who reciprocated with a *thank you* punch to the gut. He doubled onto a knee. Some freckled face kiddo laughed and pointed, hanging one-handed from the monkey bars.

The shorty said, "Marcus is done with you—making sure all the other boys in town keep you dry too. Time to move on, Buck-o. Learn from this. Grow a flower outta that piece-a-shit life of yours."

Buck stood just in time for the shorty to wipe a mustard-slathered hand across his chest. The muscle blew back to their sedan and sped off. He made for the cab. Time for Shizez.

He sat in the heap counting the wad of bills, making sure he wasn't a buck short. It was all there. The crisp bills tickled his nose as he took in a whiff of the good life. Twenty grand could give him a fresh start in any new town. Too bad, his life still wanted living.

And then it hit, crashing through his brain like the Kool-Aid man. Bobby's logic. Cal's extra twenty. He sat in contemplation, thinking it through. *Be smart!* It could work. Had to blow town though. Place was dry anyway. Taking a deep breath, he picked up the phone. Tried to say a prayer as the connection rang but forgot how.

Shizez picked up. "Got my money, bro?"

"Yeah, yeah. No problem. I got a guy set to deliver."

"When and where?"

"Pershing Square. Ten fifteen."

"Fine, but *you* deliver."

"I can't, man—but I'll be there, on the street. Marcus is tailing me—still owe him twenty. He can't see me paying you off."

"Could give a rat's cunt about Marcus, bro. Just bring me the money."

"Sure, sure—now listen up. This is how it's gonna go down…"

Star light—star bright! First star I see tonight…

Cal stood removed from the crowd, the speaker system blasting pop sensation. Carly looked adorable in her Day-Glo spandex, crimped hair and makeup. Never missing a twirl, she smiled whenever glancing in his direction. That wasn't the case with Belinda, taking in the black and blue blots under his eyes from the nose break. The step-fuck was busy, prancing around, snapping action shots center stage. Cal ignored her intense stares and relished in the moment.

Carly ran to him once it was over. He scooped her up, hoisting her high above, sunlight dancing off her platinum curls. Life didn't suck. The moment he set her down, Belinda approached, hubby in hand.

"So, what happened to your face, Cal?"

The step-fuck dawdled with his Nikon, avoiding confrontation.

Carly said, "It's makeup, Mommy. Like mine."

Cal smiled. "That's right, honey. You're *so* smart."

She giggled. "Can we get Pinkberry, Daddy?"

"I dunno. You gotta ask your mom."

Belinda picked her up and began kissing her cheek like a woodpecker.

Cal smiled until a large hand plopped on his shoulder. He spun, met by two hairy lugs clad in Euro garb.

The larger one said, "*You got something for Dookie?*"

Cal stammered. "What?"

"Whatya mean, *What*? That's the phrase for the drop. I say, *You got something for Dookie*, and then you...hand over..." He bounced his brow for a response.

Cal stood speechless. The phrase finally clicked. *Dookie.* Buck knew—a double-cross. He kept with the ignorance. "I hand over what?"

The second lug grew impatient, grabbing at his vest and pulling out the two stacks from inside. "Ya hand over the fuckin' cash, asshole—wassa matta with you?"

Cal tried to grab the cash before the first lug mangled his arm.

Belinda shot over. "What the hell is this all about?" She slapped the lugs' grip. "Let go of him."

The step-fuck intervened. "Hey, what's going on here?"

Cal and Belinda turned in unison, "Stay outta this, Glenn!"

Lug #2 counted the bills. "It's all here. Let's roll."

Belinda choked at the sight of the stacks. Carly tugged at Cal's leg as they watched the bad men walk to a limo in the distance. Parked beside it, a slime green cab. *His* cab. Cal squinted for clarity, not believing his eyes.

Buck waved out the window before peeling out, up Olive. The look on Cal's face was worth more than the wad bulging his pocket—and the cab. He laughed, thinking about the phrases he'd use when telling Bobby. Real smart like. Had at least ten hours to relive it all before hitting Albuquerque. Rest in peace, Dook. *You gotta bleed to feed* and he was stuffed like a Thanksgiving turkey. The taxi merged onto the Hollywood freeway; a neon drop in a sea of steel, gunning straight toward oblivion.

MOUTH BAY

As a child, my dreams were infinite as sunray glitter across Santa Monica Bay. I can see them all now, a legion of sparkles ignited then killed, out past the break. One flashes gymnastic glory: eight years old; summer Olympics fever. Another glimmers horseback rides through Palos Verdes bridal paths, age ten. But all those dreams died when I hit thirteen, as if stray kelp shackled my ankles, dragging me beneath crashing waves. *Was it really* love *when it came to that boy?* Then Missy: six pounds, eight ounces— nineteen inches long. I sank like a moon rock: cool, hard, weightless. That's about it for this pretty bitch—trapped in coral for so long, have to check my damn throat for gills...

"You okay there, Randi?"

Wet hands drop from my neck. "What?"

The goatee bounces. "Everythin' alright?"

I shut off the running faucet, drying with a busser's rag atop a mound of crusted forks. "Yeah...Just thinkin', Sal."

"Great...Hey, can you finish those thoughts on break? We're gettin' slammed in the ass out there."

I peer over his shoulder through crooked saloon doors. Place doesn't seem rowdy for a Friday dinner rush. Other waitresses are slouched over the bar, gazing back as if I am another rat in the kitchen. Their star-spangled bikinis clash with faux-leather chaps; hard faces masked by seven-layer dip. I swipe a mock Stetson from off a chopping block. "Sure thing—lemme just grab these hot wings for table nine. Be right out."

Wafting wing sauce burns the eyes. I saunter through tipsy old men over to a family near the John Wayne mural. Dad ogles my implants; Mom kisses her infant's hand to earn a cackle. When Missy was that tiny—couldn't remember ever taking her into restaurants. Now she's nine; rather dive into her *Goosebumps* than sit at a table in public with me. Not sure if she's embarrassed or simply going through prepubescent weirdness—either way, she'll have to deal with me same as I did her. Can't blame her. I mean, neither of us asked for this.

I sidle up to the bar, pretending to search for a customer's check. Sal is out smoking another Parliament with the new teenage hostess. I can tell she'll be in flip-flops her whole life. Beach's tractor beam takes hold of most around here. Willy gets a drink from the bartender, slides the double of Grey Goose into my hand and smacks the rose on my right butt cheek.

"Howdy, Mama."

I feign a smile, tossing a candy cane straw into the glass.

He's an old crooner, grumbling slow ballads on a stool under the big screen most nights. How he thinks he can compete with the Lakers, I'll never ask. Sings for drinks and never takes requests; by the smell of his breath, tonight began with a bang. Drives one of those custom Econolines—I caught him in a Vons parking lot once, loading his invalid wife into its rear. Tubes in her frozen face; feet gnarled as bitten taffy. Never told him about it though. Couldn't wreck his fantasy. This dump: only place he can put on for others.

I crunch an ice chip, placing a cold kiss to his brow. Janelle (the blue-haired barkeep) snaps a towel at me.

"Better get on, Rock Star. Dora's over there clearing your table."

I make a kissy face and hit the floor.

Rock Star: a blatant dig into my past. I've been called worse.

When I made it with Hank Raskin by the Wilderness Park swamp, everyone began to call me "In-N-Out." That lasted through middle school—till I met Tommy. We'd shared a joint at a Rat Beach bonfire. Everyone questioned his choice; told him of my tales, now taller than the downtown skyline. He blew 'em off—became my shield. The lead singer of Smarm. Newest band in the South Bay with a record deal. Surf punk. Members were all of seventeen. Songs about shattered homes, bones and relationships (best they knew). Backyards and basements brought notoriety. Fast living fueled egos. How was a girl not supposed to get trapped in that riptide?

Wild years slugged along. I grew entitled: backstage at every Hollywood venue, canoodling with icons, free drinks, good drugs. The title of Tommy's girlfriend was most intoxicating. I'd been faithful; too scared to ask him flat out. Not like I'd leave. Once Smarm toured Europe a third time, distance brought disaster. He was in Munich when I told him the doctor's prognosis to my sudden nausea spells. Three months in, six to go. His silence still brings chills.

The marriage lasted till Missy was two—eighteen months of which Tommy was somewhere on a bus through America. Interviews with various rock rags never came close to who he really was. I felt duped. Soon after the divorce, couldn't remember who I was anymore. Time had erased all those swells of future's promise. I live in a world where an embellished reputation defines me to others. *They don't call the South Bay "Mouth Bay" for nothing.* Twenty-six years on the run...

Had I ever been anything more than lowbrow gossip?

My shift ends. Soon as I hit the parking lot, some fucker who'd been swilling Beam near the popcorn machine tries to walk me to my car. I pretend I'm not feeling well, and he sneers in rejection. Truth is, I've felt lousy all day: stomachache/backache/headache. I'm going through the motions—no longer life's participant.

Hopefully not coming down with something sinister. Prolly need more meds.

The Cabriolet is finally paid for. Got the pink slip and everything. Cutest car *ever.* Seven long years, and I'm the proud owner of an eighteen-year-old convertible that needs new brakes. My lone accomplishment, thus far—even though my folks *did* place the down payment. A gift for getting my GED. (I cheated.) My purse rattles a pill vial tune. The sound always reminds me of those cartoon skeletons—hammering each other's dry bones like xylophones. They started me off with one vial for anxiety; ten years later, I'm basically a pharmaceutical rep. They're good to have on hand but I've never really needed 'em. Made up most my symptoms in the beginning: a foot in the door with doctors. That's the best way to land cures for pain.

I crush a Vicodin ES with my cherry lip gloss; spread it along the dash with Mom's Nordstrom card. A post-shift ritual: that Marlboro after rough sex. I gauge for nostril dregs in the rearview (Dad mentioned something, few days back). Blood neon catches my eye: *Texas Loosey's* awash down my rear plastic window.

Key turns.

Clutch sticks.

One more try, and I win.

My folks took us in when they evicted me from the Sea Breeze. Mom doesn't mind Missy; Dad calls me "The Squatter." I can still unlock the front door without clacking the bolt; any magician will tell you that a high caliber illusion (such as this) is only perfected over a thousand grand performances. Imagine what I can do after a million. Missy and I share what used to be Dad's den. Whenever my trick goes bust, she'll stir and moan, eventually cursing me for brushing my teeth with the light on. I'd ask her to come with me to the beach tomorrow, before my afternoon shift, but I'm sure she won't. Last time she wore Dr. Martens and draped herself in black denim while I baked evenly in the sun. I swear if it wasn't for *me,* we'd get pegged as outsiders—sand poachers from Hawthorne or Lomita. Hey, I didn't suffer the torments of this place to be anything but a local! Christ. One day Missy'll fucking get it.

My stomach howls. I haven't eaten anything but yogurt today. Mom's reading something romantic at the kitchen table, sipping her chamomile tea. She stopped coloring her hair last year for some reason. Wisps of grey streak here and there; the mother who raised me wouldn't have left the house in curlers. I hope one day I too can let go—get lost in some trashy love realm made up of greased abs and veiny biceps. I'm careful not to make a peep, knowing how Mom gets when she's immersed. Her eyes scan a page as if I'm some specter passing through. I dig at a familiar itch on my nose. She knows I'm out of it but doesn't harp. Gave up on me after the last rehab—told me I was merely a headstone in this family. Pretty sure she turned to the dark side after I got caught breaking into houses, pawning any score for pills or worse. *My little illusion can open most doors.* Needless to say, police station/jail visits wear on parents. I don't blame her. She slurps a gulp and says to me, "We ate Ruby's earlier—no leftovers. Haven't gone shopping either."

I put a little sugar in my voice. "'Kay, Mom." A jar of pickles waves at me when I open the fridge.

"Missy needs new reading glasses, you know?"

My eyelids fall. "'Kay."

"The pair she liked was a hundred twenty."

"Well, I get paid next week, so…"

"Oh, I already bought them for her. I'm telling you how much you owe us."

I close the refrigerator gently and head back to the den, crunching into the pickle as if it were a live pigeon.

Can't remember a summer in Redondo ever being this humid. Thick, sticky—like breathing through a crazy straw. Zero waves, longboarders speckling the coast in denial. Beachgoers remind me of ants on a hill. Good thing I can still kill a bikini. I'm tan all year for this reason alone. Missy didn't want to come with me so I called up my one girlfriend (Donna). I don't have to be at work till four. We're meeting on the pier for daiquiris and a man hunt. Haven't seen anyone in weeks that gets us wet, but we love talking shit and damn good at it too.

My roller skates were once pristine: creamy suede, bubblegum pink wheels. That was when Tommy got 'em for me one Christmas, twelve years ago. Prolly shouldn't wear them anymore but I can't afford a new pair (thanks to Missy). They have more mileage than the Cabriolet, easily. Everyone I know who rides skates has broken their tailbone at least once. Not this girl. It's a simple glide that I've perfected over the years, nearly effortless on The Strand's sleek concrete. I am grace incarnate upon spinning polyurethane, swinging my arms with a fluidity that swishes my glistening bust for all to see. Dudes must think I was a professional ice skater at one time—an athlete— someone important. I pretend like I don't notice their stares, but I see 'em, love 'em—slurp 'em up for breakfast!

Barney's Beanery is the newest haunt on the second tier of the Redondo Pier. I used to go to the original in West Hollywood whenever Tommy played the Troubadour. Be surprised if this one lasts longer than the previous pub. Doesn't matter. Some other lush den will take its place. All it takes is for locals to turn their backs (which is a given), and then I have a peaceful hangout till the place files for bankruptcy.

I sling my skates over a shoulder and hit the patio. Donna is giggling in a booth, fluffing a waiter barely out his teens. Behind her, the Pacific is cold and tepid. She's my best friend, but I couldn't tell you her exact age or what neighborhood she grew up in. An army brat from Vegas, I think. Used to work Loosey's with me before they caught her skimming tips. She's nearly twice my size (in weight not height). Used to be a double threat, but last year she let her ass turn into a deformed pumpkin; now the girl has to squeeze into tops that'll make her tits defy gravity. Donna's a perfect companion for clubbing or daytime drinks, such as this. When someone walks by us—*anyone*—I get off on knowing exactly who they're looking at. Let's be honest, the girl reads *books,* okay? We could never be true BFFs.

The waiter seems startled by my kissy face as I nudge his elbow with my right breast, sliding into the booth. Donna blows me an air smooch. Her face looks like a corn puff: She's been drinking for days.

I fucking love this bitch!

Donna chugs a craft brew as I flick my tongue on a daiquiri straw. She ordered some fried mac-n-cheese bites "for us." She's halfway through her latest date horror when I catch a familiar face down below. Willy is pushing his twisted wife past the churro stand. The woman looks different from this angle, like a squirmy larvae stuck in a peach. I feel for him. Least, I try to. Could've sworn the woman was Asian, but from here she is obviously white. Something about being a voyeur always makes me giddy. Willy looks awkward as hell in his dumb cowboy gear. *What the hell is he doing with that poor crip in public?* I've heard him sing a thousand tunes and not one was about this burden.

Donna clears her throat as the appetizer arrives.

"Sorry, babe. What were you saying?"

Donna wolfs a cheese bite and starts back in. I tune her out, deciding that drinks with her today was a bad idea. She'll die alone but refuses to accept it. Why should I have to listen to her pathetic whine? I pretend that my phone buzzed and peer into my purse.

"Oh, shit."

"What is it?"

"Nothin'. Forgot about something I need to do. *Fuck.*" I tap my acrylics on the cocktail glass before sucking its dregs. "Sorry. I gotta go, hun. Drinks on me next time, 'kay? I'll text." Before Donna can speak through another mouthful, I shoot out the booth with an eyes-closed kissy face and rush for the stairs.

I keep my distance nearing the break wall. A double scoop of fat-free rainbow sherbet helps to conceal my face, doubling as lunch. Willy and his wife are at a far bench, taking in the grandeur of sailboats cutting the bay. I should rephrase that: Willy is seated at the bench while his wife remains in her wheelchair, doing her impression of a dolphin caught in a tuna net.

Don't say it.

I already know.

I'm sooo bad.

A drip of ice cream falls between my tits and sends a jolt. I almost yelp but don't want to blow my cover. I spin in a circle, tossing the cone to some gulls in the harbor. That's when I can hear her sobbing. Was this just her daily cry—the wail of the wretched? I could do a dozen pouty frowns right now, but I won't. Salt breeze has me imagining the taste of her tears. *Willy, you poor old fool.*

Maybe it's all the pills, but I kind of feel detached, you know? Last time I cried was when Bowie died—but even then, I merely capitalized on an opportunity. Seeing their display makes me sick. Still can't imagine letting someone into my heart *that* close.

Fool me once, cruel world—

There's a little pep in my step tonight, shuttling baby back ribs and Coke refills to hearty eaters, facedown in their plates. They snort like hounds given people food. The only thing that would make this job worse would be if humans devoured their dinner like flies; a cacophony of slurps and regurgitation instead of the usual mindless banter or family feud. Willy is perched on his stool before a mic, grinding away at his guitar; his boot taps to the beat of an old Hank tune. Some days he sounds pretty good. I pause in the kitchen to take in the song, reliving that pier-side visual of him and his wife. A creeping headache at the base of my skull lets me know a migraine is coming on. I rub my neck but hear Sal approaching with the new girl and act like I'm busy loading napkins. Saloon doors swing, letting in a sea of giggles. I turn toward them, a sour look on my face to show something's wrong. Sal lets me take an early break. I'm positive he's about to fuck this little slut in his office.

Believe me.

I would know.

The smoker's patio is empty. I contemplate rushing to the Cabriolet to snort a rail but then remember I'm fresh out of Vics. The migraine could be the beginnings of withdrawal, but I pretend it's from stress. The menthol barely hits my lips before the door swings open and out walks Willy with his Zippo. I don't have to ask: his flame is always mine. We smoke in silence for three puffs. His face is much more weathered under the moon's spell. I'm sure I'd cry too if I could see myself in this light.

"I liked that song."

"Which, dear?"

"Dunno what it's called." I hum a few bars and say the only lyrics I recall.

Willy smiles, wrinkles on his face climbing like torn leather. "'Lovesick Blues.' Yeah, that one'll haunt."

Mid-drag, a needle jolts my brain. I wince, and he notices.

"Everythin' alright?"

"Migraine." I drop the smoke to rub my temples.

Willy looks over his shoulder before pulling out a small tin case from his pocket. He opens it, presenting it to me like some engagement ring. "One a these ought to kill it."

With a simple glance, I know exactly what pills they are: little devils that got me into my first stint of rehab. Tommy introduced them to me when I flew out to see him gig Brooklyn. They're pretty hard to come by nowadays. Heroin is much cheaper and that's what sent me spiraling the last time. "Where'd you get these?"

"My wife needs 'em. She suffers from chronic pain—after the accident."

I want to ask about this *accident*, but then I'd have to swallow the pool of saliva I've already gathered to munch this beast. The moment its bitterness caresses my tongue, it's like an old friend back to visit.

There's no going back now.

I'm done for.

"Thanks."

He returns the case to his back pocket. "Don't mention it, girl. Always got plenty 'round the house for my sweet Missy."

"Missy? That your wife's name?"

"Yeah."

"That's my daughter's name."

He exhales a plume. "I didn't know you had a child."

"Yeah, well…" I move for the door and tickle his shoulder with my nails. "Thanks again, Willy."

The world is rosy once again. I scratch my nose, taking in the barroom panorama of gnashing teeth and gnarled faces. Sal's not going to like me asking to go home early, but I don't care. An idea has popped into my brain that is clawing like a cornered lobster. I crash saloon doors, through the kitchen and punch into the main office. The new girl is half-clothed and seated on Sal's desk chair. She's been crying (a lot); Sal looks like he's trying to sell her a used car. I tell him my plight, and he doesn't even wince. Protecting his ass in this situation is far more important than little ole me. I toss my apron at one of the fry cooks and hit the bricks.

* * *

Donna's down as fuck, so I give her a call. She agrees to meet me at my parents' house: I told her I felt horrible about leaving her today and want to make it up to her. She has no idea what I've got in store.

I pull the Cabriolet into the driveway and hope that none of the house's upstairs lights click on. Luckily, I keep my illusion kit in the glovebox. Don't ask why...I mean, you can imagine. Looks like my old rig case back when I was really hooked; the insides can pick any basic door lock. Hopefully, I won't need to use it. I mean, a knock with this face behind the door is usually good enough. At least, it used to get me backstage when Tommy stopped putting me on the VIP list.

Donna pulls up in her lifted Ford pickup. I eye the house one more time before darting into the street and climbing into the cab. I have a strange feeling that Missy saw me; her curtain shimmered. I block it out. Donna hightails it; I don't even have to ask.

Willy plays another set in six minutes, so I'll have all the time I need. I navigate Donna through a zigzag of charmless homes off Anza and Sepulveda. That time I saw Willy in the Vons parking lot, I guess I forgot to mention that I followed him in the Cabriolet for most of the day. I like to watch, remember? His house is a modest one-story slathered in bright lavender paint. Home Depot must've had it on clearance or something. Donna parks across the street as I eye the darkened curtains for any sign of life.

"What's going on, Randi?"

"Lemme see your purse."

I remember that she carries this pink stun gun wherever she goes. I swipe it and open the door. The scent of wet grass floats into the cab. I realize this girl deserves some sort of explanation—

at least a reason not to ditch me. "I gotta collect some money this bitch owes me. Once I get it, we can go party, 'kay? Don't worry. Everything'll be fine."

"I really gotta pee."

My eyes remain still, but I feel them rolling back into my skull. I can tell by her glassy eyes that a party is already coursing her veins. She must've kept throwing 'em back at Barney's all day. "Pinch it a little longer, girl. I'll be right quick." I march over Willy's front lawn, destroying a row of petunias. To think Donna drove her truck to pick *me* up in her current state drives me nuts. *What a selfish whore.* I decide not to knock; if the wretch is inside, I'm pretty sure she can't open a goddamn door. I unzip the illusion kit.

Alakazam!

Inside the house it is completely dark, curtains drawn, not even a sliver of moonlight. Smells like my grandpa's last hospital room—the time when Mom made me sit with him while she ran out for a doctor. Can still see that dry tongue spilling out his face. *Just another of life's bad tattoos.* In a far bedroom I can hear a TV blaring: some talent show with a famous Stones tune being molested. I smack my shin on a poorly placed coffee table and bite down on my lip to prevent an expletive. *Never been in a living room without couches before; prolly from the wheelchair.* Blue light begins to flicker down the hallway. Stun gun in hand, I unlock its safety and wait for a courage that never comes. Thirty seconds feels like hours. I still don't hear a peep—too shaky to check. The wretch is either asleep or captivated by some poor singer about to have his world shattered. I slide the gun into a back pocket and head for the bathroom.

The cabinet above the sink is filled with medical supplies and some tube inscribed *Analpram.* I wince and head for the kitchen. Mom used to hide her Percocet from me atop our refrigerator. I figure it's a safe bet to search before storming into that bedroom as if it were Black Friday. I tiptoe across linoleum and spot an entire Rubbermaid box filled with beautiful amber vials beside the microwave. Goose flesh tingles up the arms, surging onwards to my ears. My itchy nose smells victory.

I attack, careful not to rattle each treasure. This twisted bitch has got it all. I could die happy swallowing one pastel tablet after another; pretty little coffins meant to solve everything—all for *me*! At first, I start to open each but think better. I'm about to glom the whole case when I hear the front door creak open.

I freeze.

A whisper cracks the world.

"Baby girl...I gotta pee."

Fucking Donna! I rush to shush her. That's when I hear it: the end of that horrid song out the TV. Donna is holding her crotch like a toddler; *bitch is good for nothing*. I put a finger to my lips and wave her back outside. She defies me, rushing into the hallway, searching for a bathroom. Her boots click atop wood flooring. I rush after her. Soon as I lunge into the hallway, the far bedroom door opens, illuminating the walls. A Latina in scrubs emerges; in her hands, a bag of BBQ Lay's. The sight of me forces a scream from deep inside her.

Why didn't I check the fucking room?

Of course, this crip has a nurse when left alone!

I reach for the great equalizer in my back pocket. The girl shoots into the bedroom, slamming the door, locking it shut.

I turn to the kitchen.

The plan is now to grab that case and leave Donna to her own devices. Her piss stream from out the bathroom is like a lion's roar in my ears. I take one lunge backwards and slam into the hallway doorframe. My back pocket ignites, turning the world into a brilliant supernova. I am paralyzed, timbering to the floor. I can see but can't focus—does that make any sense? Something shoots up at me—cracks my neck before I can even pound the ground. *Goddamn coffee table!*

Relief washes greater than high tide.

All pain is killed, consciousness lost.
I am a moon rock.
I feel nothing.

For a life billed as lowbrow gossip, I can only imagine what *Mouth* Bay thinks of me now. Sure as hell isn't Rock Star. The coma was induced but I'm pretty sure I would've pulled through. I mean, I always have before. Take it from me: Hack doctors always jack up their hospital tab. *Whatever.* I'm covered for now thanks to Texas Loosey's; Dad'll put up the house if he has to—at least that's what Mom said. Missy brings me flowers most days but still can't even pull it together to look me in the eyes. I don't blame her. I have yet to gaze into a mirror.

Well, it's not that easy: I can't without being propped.

"From the neck down" is all I remember them saying once I woke up. Can still see that supernova whenever I close my eyes; then again, this cocktail they have me on is the best I've ever tasted. Almost feel my extremities. I smirk thinking that Missy'll call *me* The Wretch from here on out, our caretaking roles now reversed. Oh, shit. I just remembered that Willy's wife's named Missy too. She won't call me a damn thing, since she can't speak. Sometime's life's a pisser. I'll talk again, they think. Willy decided not to file charges after hearing of my perpetual state. What a softy. Donna on the other hand—never mind...Who fucking cares about that whore? *I'm done for—and so is she—so are all of us!*

The cute RN delivers some apple juice and presses the straw to my dry tongue. His forearms are all veiny like the guys in Mom's trashy novels. I'm sure he had his way with me when I was out cold—I mean, why wouldn't he? I'd let him do it again too. Spread these gams right now if I could, see if I can feel his pressure. *A new illusion to master.* On a more uplifting note, I've lost eighteen pounds!

The RN's attention begins to drift to another patient's call.

Here comes the best part of my day.
I think about never roller skating again and squeeze out a
tear. It bombs onto the blue gown tenting my bust. The RN
jumps into action, swiping its trail from off my cheek.
To feel his coarse finger almost makes this all worth it.
It's all so simple now, letting go.
One daily cry, and I win.

VIN SCULLY EYES

I.

If the Torrance Costco would've just had the *right* damn pickles, Montrose Laughlin III wouldn't have had to stifle his day, driving Mother's beloved Jag twenty minutes outside his comfort zone to visit the Long Beach Costco. Although, it wasn't as if he had any real plans—like most days. The inconvenience was what irked. Surely, the Torrance store's employees had taken notice every time he trudged inside (first day of every month) to re-stock his cabinets for another thirty days. And he *always* bought *multiple* four-packs of monster hot and sour dills—couldn't live without them—and now, today of all days, they hadn't the foresight to replenish their goddamn load. For certain, the world was playing a fine cruel joke.

The San Diego Freeway was crammed, inching along, bumper to bumper—no longer functional in its design for modern vehicles. Mother's Jaguar hadn't been on any freeway in over two decades, a garaged beauty fit for coastal cruises or a night on the town. She'd be inflamed at the thought of her only son cruising her "baby" into the bowels of Los Angeles on such a laughable task. But she couldn't react one bit, not from the mantel she was perched on back home—her gold urn, cold and unamused as her lifelong gaze. The Jag's engine revved in place. Monty huffed in defeat, searching the radio for any sign of sports talk, it being midseason when baseball trades shook the world.

He arrived at the Costco thirty minutes later than it should've taken, exiting the car and charging a bay of carts. By the clothes on his mousy frame, one never would've pegged him as an heir to a real estate fortune. When Mother passed, he gave up on appearances, one thing she had an iron-grip on throughout his youth. Private school uniforms. Apparel for every season in matching hues. The last time he'd purchased sneakers was in 1997: Air Jordans (black/red/white), an entire crate, size nine. Same with baggy denim and loud T-shirts. Mass quantities of comfort that he didn't care looked dated nowadays.

Mother's ghost just grabbed her chest.

For a Tuesday afternoon, the store seemed tranquil. Layout looked to be nearly identical to Torrance, so he headed through stacks of processed foods, toward giant canisters and condiment buckets. Eight pallets ahead, on the left, sat the pickled goods. The sight of that pink pig on every jar nearly sparked flatulence. He loaded up the cart, buying triple his usual, just in case Torrance couldn't get their shit together. After free samples of sausage and a long line at the register, he was back on the road for home.

With the 405 still a mess, Monty navigated streets, hoping to open the Jag's engine down Willow till it morphed into Sepulveda. Hadn't been outside the South Bay in so long, almost forgot what the real world looked like. Everything was in decline: roads, buildings. The violet pedals on jacarandas even appeared to be weeping. He revved to a stop at Long Beach Boulevard; the looks on other drivers' faces had him wishing he'd raised the convertible's roof. A hearty voice called to him from the center median. He craned to see a large black gentleman holding a sign with a picture of a teen flashing his gold teeth. The poster blared, FUNERAL DONATIONS 4 LIL MEEZY.

"Anythin' will help us, sir. My son. Firstborn—only twenty-three an' taken back to God's glory." The man pointed across to the far median. "Two young girls ova dere his keeds. Four an' nine."

Monty scanned the intersection, watching other poster-clad family members walk up and down car lanes, pleading for compassion, scooping an occasional dollar. The light flashed green. Monty returned to the man, meeting his crystal gaze. "Sorry. No cash."

Before, "God bless," could leave the poor man's lips, Monty's engine charged west.

II.

Lamont Craig II decided he'd had enough for today, soon as that pricey foreign roadster left him penniless, flying down Willow—its driver a disheveled shell of a man. He guzzled a large Gatorade from out a cooler in the rear of his "work truck"—a '92 Suburban with magnets across its body that read:

CRAIG ELECTRICAL CO.
You've been Had by The Rest. Now try The Best!
1-888-GO-CRAIG

His wife, Eloise, was fanning off his granddaughters with a newspaper beside him, misting water above their beaded braids. Their faces were painful to take in, two pairs of his dead son's eyes beaming back. He handed the bottle to his remaining son (Trey, eighteen), busy counting donations they'd gathered before the heat beat them down. "What it do?"

"Made like two hunny."

Lamont reflected, adding the total for the past two days in his mind: $520. A drop in the bucket—the urn for what they needed to send his boy to heaven right. There was no savings to dip, no retirement plan to plunder. This was all a bad dream, aftershocks in play for the rest of his days.

How could his boy be gone in a whisper?

Eloise loaded the girls into the car, its insides finally cool enough to buckle them. The men climbed inside. As Lamont drove home, the blank looks off every person he approached in that intersection churned the brain. Never mind what they *thought*: another dead thug on the ghetto streets. To them his boy was probably just some hood that deserved what he got. *But he didn't*. No one earned the right to be on the wrong side of a bullet—no matter who they were. And Lamont Craig III—Meezy to the homies—was his son. His blood...taken out like a rabid dog for wearing the wrong color shoes. He sparked a Marlboro 100 to vanquish them all, those dumb stares, ghosts out his lungs into a blistering sun.

Eloise and the girls gently wept in the back seat; Trey handed over fresh Kleenex as the Suburban pulled into the driveway of their weathered abode. Couldn't remember the lawn ever being green or window bars not rusted. His brother would often joke about the place, calling it The Kennel, often met by Father's sneer; Pop's knees had been obliterated by years spent crawling floors, wiring nicer homes in better neighborhoods so his family could eek out this life. One thing was certain: There was no way he'd be another stooge on his knees when *he* grew up. Life was one big hustle, either the moon or the gutter, and Trey wasn't going to gamble on something better—he would achieve it—become a professional in this world. He'd already killed the SATs and been accepted to two private colleges. Wasn't like he was in line for any grants or scholarships though. The plan was to hit Long Beach Community for his undergrad; hopefully by then, he could save enough working for Pops and take out a loan to help make that dream a reality. But there was one major caveat: He wouldn't be taking over the family business, like his brother was supposed to—and that wouldn't be tolerated by

Pops. Shit, just going to community college got met with a chuckle by the old man. With this sudden death in the family, that dream would have to be a secret from now on.

The room he shared with Junior had cracks in the walls covered by pictures of Gang Starr and Tribe. (He never called him Meezy. He was Junior since day one—no matter what the streets claimed.) Band posters were all that Momma would allow, never tolerating big titties or butt cracks inside her home. He opened the closet, staring at Junior's blue wardrobe, taking out a puffy Dodgers jacket and sniffing it, burying emotion deep inside. He slid it on in front of the mirrored door. His hands dug into the pockets, right one hit something cold, hard. Instantly, he knew what it was, slowly pulling out the revolver, noticing it was loaded.

The fuck, Junior?

When did it all go south?

He opened a high drawer, one used for socks and undies, burying the Smith & Wesson deep inside. He wondered how much it'd fetch on the street. *Could buy a haul of textbooks.* Knew exactly who to approach: Kermit. Tomorrow they were going down to the funeral home too—same one Kermit's dad owned. He'd probably be there, working. Kermit ran with a questionable crew, like most boys out here. Surely, he'd know someone that needed a piece—hell, maybe even himself. Trey took another glance in the mirror before tearing off the jacket and kicking it into the closet.

III.

A brisk, salty breeze welcomed Monty back to Manhattan Beach, ocean a snoring beast in the distance. To think his great-grandfather had the foresight to purchase large swaths of acreage up this coast many years ago; Monty still held title to several homes and businesses throughout the community. Would've had more if Mother hadn't begun selling off parcels to eager socialites and celebrities throughout the '70's. Didn't really matter though—not like he had any children or other family to pass the fortune. If he ever got short of money, he'd just sell a home for five to ten million and go on with his humdrum ways. There were no worries in store for Monty, so when the issue of a potential new neighbor moving in next door became a possibility, it tilted his barge.

ESPN radio had no reports of any Dodger players being traded yet. Monty felt a short relief wash over as the Jag climbed up his narrow driveway, then descended into a subterranean garage. The home was originally built as a two-story, back when his father still controlled the acreage between it and the coast. Upon his passing, after Mother's selling spree to uphold her gilded existence, the home was demolished and rebuilt to accommodate four stories, cementing a panoramic view above all who'd built downhill. Monty rarely even visited the first two stories, now converted into storage, filled with Mother's artifacts from her global escapades and priceless paintings sheathed in plastic. He rode the elevator up, arms heavy with pickle jars. Approaching the kitchen, a sound of the television brought concern. In the living room sat his best and only friend, his neighbor—a relief pitcher for the "Boys in Blue" named Robbie Slate.

"Elle's having another one of her Real Housewife parties. Had to bail, man. You don't mind, right?"

Monty tossed him a beer can from out the fridge.

Robbie caught it with his right arm—the left shackled in an intricate brace from a recent labral tear procedure.

"My place is your place—why I gave you that emergency key. You didn't have a problem with the new security system, right? Same code."

"Nah, it was cool. What'd you do to it?"

"Upgraded the surveillance—smaller cameras. Guess I just got bored with the old one. They're coming out next week to set up the exterior."

"You don't have outdoor cameras?"

"I do, but the monitor's busted. Wear and tear."

Robbie popped the can with his teeth and sniffed its contents.

"This a new South Bay brew or what?"

"Nah, they've been 'round a few years. Harbortown Ales. Specialize in Belgians but this is their unfiltered Citra DIPA. Drink it."

Robbie swilled. "Tastes like oranges...grapefruit even."

"People are going ape shit for it—camping out along Western."

"Fuckin' delicious. You buying in?"

"I've made it known that I'm willing to invest. They're all young though. Kids. The brew master ain't out his twenties. See what happens, but yeah...I want in." He cracked his own can. "Heard you haven't been placed on the chopping block yet."

"Who told you that?"

"Radio. If you get traded, wanna sell your house back to me?"

"Fuck no. We'll rent in whatever shit city they send me."

"*If* you get traded."

"Yeah...*if.*"

"Think it'll happen?"

"Fuck if I know. My numbers were solid, before..." He raised his broken wing.

"What the doc say?"

"I'm on ice for at least ten months—best case scenario. Anyway, if I don't hear from my agent by midnight tomorrow, I'm good for another season."

He plopped on the couch, admiring a yacht in the bay.

"Lemme ask you something, Monty."

"Shoot."

"*Beer,* you serious? Why don't you put money in real estate— I mean, it's in your blood, bro?"

"Golden Road just sold to Budweiser for nearly a billion. How's beer not lucrative these days? I own enough property as it is."

"I'm talking new developments. Have you been in downtown lately?"

He laughed. "No."

"Elle and I were at this charity function the other night—"

"What charity?"

"Some foundation for the blind—or maybe it was prostate cancer. Shit, I'm at so many of these things, I lose track."

Monty reflected on the last time he ever did anything nice for anyone other than himself. *Charity?* He should try it one of these days.

"What was I saying?"

"Downtown."

"Yeah, so, we're at this dinner at the Ritz—I'm gazing out the windows, taking in the view. Fuckin' cranes galore, man. Every corner has something new going up—and I mean *up*—high in the sky. Most of the designs are batshit too. Everyone's got a boner for Frank Gehry, right? So, then it hits me. *The Future.*"

"Future smacked you in the face?"

"Kinda. *Marvels* are being built, man. Mini metropolises. Giant works of art. Live/Work/Play. Condo owners never have to venture out their building's grounds. That's when it hits me—this is the future of Los Angeles. Build some giant campus—a contained city within the City, make it shaped like something weird—a legion of colliding locomotives or some shit. Next door, a developer builds another, even more outlandish—the view out every unit window framing another 3-D Dali built across the way. That's the future. Build 'em high and keep folks dumb—drunk on steel. I've already got my accountant reaching out to developers, ones moving into South Central. Never been done before in the history of L.A. The future is now, and if you don't buy in, you're gonna miss out, man."

Monty snickered into his beer.

"That funny to you? Think I'm crazy, right? I'm not."

"No, I feel you. It's just—"

"Just what?"

"My father used to always say *the future* depended on investing in children—their livelihood...education."

"Whose children? You an' I don't have any dogs in that race."

"I know but kids own the future—can't argue with that—even ones that brew beer." By the twist on Robbie's face, the concept was lost, so Monty refrained. "Forget it. That's a good idea though—yours. I'm sure you'll make a killing."

"Damn right."

"'Nother beer?"

"Please. Hey, you should come with Elle and me to the next event. She thinks you look generous. Always says you got them Vin Scully eyes. Very kind."

Monty headed for the kitchen, smiling. "Don't know about that, but Elle's an angel for thinking." The word *charity* flashed like neon in his brain.

Why hadn't he entertained it earlier?

He knew the answer, it reflected back at him, eye to eye in the sleek refrigerator door. "Maybe I'll take you up on that offer. Come here, check this out."

Robbie rose from the couch and joined Monty before a ceramic nude bust of a female torso, hanging at the hallway entrance. "That's cool, man. *Erotica*. New?"

"Yeah. See anything weird about it?"

Robbie analyzed the bust. "Nah."

Monty switched off the hall lights. Inside the ivory nipples were pinpoint red dots.

"No way. New security cameras?"

Monty nodded. "These spy minis are all over. Pretty cool, right?"

"Shit, yeah. Maybe the home security market is where to invest?"

"Possibly...or else we just keep on living our dang lives."

Monty smiled as Robbie mimed slurping an areola.

***

Next morning, the Jag pulled into an industrial corridor just north of Old Town Torrance. The Strand Brewing Co. was located inside a large warehouse where craft beer was brewed and bottled on a daily basis. Monty retrieved two amber growlers from out his trunk and walked inside to have them filled. The tasting room staff didn't know him very well, but they knew *of* him—word through the beer community about some stiff with deep pockets, hoping to pay to play in their business. He sipped a pint of pale while his bottles were filled, sitting at a picnic bench, scrolling through his cell to see Robbie's trade status. Looked like his neighbor was safe for now, their conversation yesterday keeping Monty awake for part of the night. He *should* do something positive with his inheritance. An act that would cost little to him but change someone's life for the better. Fuck real estate, that empty void often displaced those truly in need. A random monetary donation would be like tossing a stone into a lake, watching the ripples, knowing that he made the impact. He'd start off small, maybe pay for someone's groceries or write a check to a soup kitchen or…

What would Vin do?

The beerback called his name; he approached for both growlers. The moment his fingers touched that icy brew, it hit him like a crisp jab.

Yesterday: *that family with the funeral!*

A grin climbed his face as he rushed to the Jag and peeled out the lot.

The intersection mirrored the day before, family members at every median in the ninety-degree heat. Monty spotted the father at the southerly light; he hooked a right down Long Beach and cut a quick U, heading back to Willow. The father looked in his direction, but upon seeing him, turned and headed back to a foldout chair set up with an umbrella. Monty honked to get the man's attention. Soon as he craned, Monty waved him over.

IV.

Lamont leaned Meezy's poster to his chair and approached the foreign roadster, thinking, *Fuck this white fool want?* Grin on the dude's face was waxy—kind he'd seen in a hundred horror movies. Before he could open his mouth, the man spoke.

"I'd like to have a word with you."

"'Bout what?"

"This whole production you got here."

"*Production?*" Lamont sneered. "Get the hell on witchoo."

"I mean no disrespect—that came out wrong."

"Ya think?"

"I wanna help. Can we talk somewhere?"

Lamont scanned the intersection; Trey was giving him a look, wondering what was going on. He waved him over. The light turned green. "Meet me in the parking lot—over there," he pointed, "beside that Suburban."

Trey's face remained blank, wondering who this white man was in the vintage Air Jordans, along with his agenda. By the frozen look on Pop's face, figured the old man held the same thought.

Monty stood silent for a beat, wondering if they'd misheard him. "Said I'd like to cover the costs...for the funeral—all of 'em."

Lamont: "May I ask why? I mean yesterday you—"

"That's just it. Yesterday got me thinking. Seeing your family out here, that picture of your son—couldn't recall the last time I ever helped anyone beside myself. Look Laah...what was it again?"

"Lamont. This here is my son, Trey."

"Lamont. Trey. Nice to meet you. I know this may sound bizarre, and I understand your tentative reaction, but hear me out. My name is Monty Laughlin. I'm a lifelong Angeleno from Manhattan Beach who is capable of erasing the financial burden of your tragedy. That's all there is to it. There are no hidden fees with this offer or monetary gain seen on my behalf—only the satisfaction of knowing that I did something positive today—helping Lil Meezy get a proper burial. Now...all you gotta do is say yes, and we can get started."

"I'll need to speak with my wife first."

"Sure thing. I'll wait." He watched as Lamont walked to the rear of the Suburban, tractor beamed by his spouse's hungry eyes.

Trey stayed put. "You serious about all this, Monty?"

"Cross my heart. Can I ask what happened to your brother?"

"Got shot outside a strip club—Fantasy Castle—over in Signal Hill."

"*Jesus*. I saw that in the *Times*. They catch the bastard responsible?"

"Nope. Never do. Say, what you do for a living?"

"I'm in between things at the moment. Guess you could call me a...beer man."

"Beer? What, like Bud Ice or somethin'?"

"Craft beer—West Coast IPAs mostly. I'm trying to invest in local breweries." The kid looked at him as if he were speaking French.

Lamont returned with his wife and grandkids.

Monty said, "Well?"

The woman let go of the children's hands and walked up to him, a glimmer in both eyes. For some reason, Monty had the feeling she was about to slap him. Before he could flinch, the woman wrapped both arms around his ribs and began to sob.

They insisted Monty come to their home for lunch; after all, they needed to discuss moving forward with his help. Trey asked to ride along with him in the Jag, helping guide the way. Monty couldn't believe this turn of events, a simple decision having him feeling completely alive.

"You're going to have to park this car in our driveway. Believe me. You don't want it out on the street."

Monty surveyed the neighborhood, his jovial feeling subsiding with every awkward glance by young men draped in blue, loitering on corners or smoking on front porches. The sight of their home struck him oddly, its deferred state. To Monty, the place was condemnable. He parked where Trey recommended, not having the gumption to tell the boy that this car meant as much to him as finding a heads-up penny.

He humored his way through a lunch of leftover soul food, the dish both warm and comforting. A Black Jesus cast judgment upon him, crucified to a far wall. A matching Last Supper hung near the dining table. He grubbed as the couple let on. Lamont and Eloise had already picked out a funeral home they would use, a friend's business. Still up for discussion was the proper urn for their child's ashes. Lamont slid him a brochure with some modest-looking urns, nothing close to the grandeur of Mother's golden vessel.

Monty slid back the brochure. "Why don't we head on down there and see what else they have. I want everyone to be satisfied."

Lamont smiled at Eloise, taking off her apron. "Well, they were expecting us to swing by today."

Monty wiped off with a napkin. "Great. What's the address?"

Trey: "I'll roll with you. Lemme just grab my phone and meet you out front." He sprinted into the bedroom, opening the closet and retrieving the pistol from Junior's jacket.

V.

The crematorium was located amongst a stretch of dilapidated commercial and industrial buildings, the last functioning business on the whole damn block. Monty counted liquor stores and USMC billboards the whole way there. Once he parked the car in the lot, Trey began to giggle.

"What is it?"

"Nothin'. Just your getup is all. You realize what kinda shoes you're wearing, right?"

"Jordans, man—come on. I love these shoes. Now you're gonna goof on me?"

"Goof? Nah. Them kicks be worth a lot a cash, dog. Jordan eights. Saw a pair online go for over five hunny."

"No shit?"

"True."

"Well, then I guess I made a smart investment, huh? What size you wear?"

Trey perked. "Twelve."

"These are size nine. Bummer."

Trey squinted, contemplating a biblical gesture. "Were you just about to give me the shoes off your feet?"

Monty killed the engine. "*What?* No. Just asked 'cause I have about twenty pair in their original boxes, back home. Bought them in bulk in '97. Would've given you a pair, if they fit. Bummer, right?"

"Damn straight."

They exited, Suburban pulling into a slot beside them. Trey watched the interaction between Monty and his parents; the man was some kind of genie, one they never summoned.

Monty chummed it up with the head of the mortuary, a skeletal black fellow named Isaiah. They exchanged pleasantries, ones appropriate for such a setting. Upon closer inspection of the grounds, the funeral home didn't look to be financially solvent: ceiling water damage, torn carpeting—not even a secretary to answer the bereaved. Place didn't do custom urns either, like Mother's. Lamont and Eloise were stuck surveying a shelf of copper urns till Monty pointed at some featuring higher-end precious metals. Isaiah jumped in to describe each of their fine attributes. There being only two variants meant this place hardly sold them. A young man came in from the back room. Monty watched as Trey slapped hands with the kid—a deep scar on his chin like one found on a flawed pumpkin. The boys headed outside. Focusing back on the task at hand, it was easy to see which urn Eloise wanted for her son—she just wouldn't say it, caressing cold silver like a newborn. Monty tapped Isaiah's shoulder: "We'll take it. I'd like to cut a check for the total sum as well, including cremation, et cetera. Do you accept checks?"

The man's eyes turned devilish; his broken smile could've split the world.

The boys took cover behind a tall dumpster at the rear of the building. As Kermit perused the weapon, Trey kept his eye on the parking lot in case his parents and Monty came strolling out. Kermit snapped the cylinder, sniping down the barrel as if he'd ever shot one of these before. Maybe he had; Trey didn't care to ask, only thing on his mind being book money.

"So, what you think?"

The scar on Kermit's chin frowned. "Got bullets?"

Trey dug out the original six from his pocket. "Jus' a starter kit. They sell 'em at Big Five."

"I know that." Kermit handled the ammo. "How much you say again?"

"Got wax in them ears, bruh? Four hunny." Trey had done his research online and knew the gun was, at best, a two Benjamin steal. Now he sat back to see if Kermit had done his own homework, banking the kid hadn't when it came to high school. "Hey, you guys toss body parts in here?" His knuckle knocked the dumpster.

"What? No." Kermit flinched at Trey, jutting his arms out like a zombie. "Quit playin'."

Trey smirked.

"Listen, this piece ain't for me, okay? It's for my boy—"

"Don't tell me his name. I don't wanna know nothin' 'bout

nothin'."

"Well, he ain't gonna pay you four hunny—I can tell ya that."

"So what then?"

"Three."

"Fiddy"

"Twenny-five."

Trey stuck out his hand. Kermit shook it, removing a wad of twenties from out a hip pocket slouched beside his kneecap. He counted the bills. "Who dat white fool witchoo?"

"Jus' some dude. He's paying for Junior's funeral."

"Junior?"

"Meezy."

"Fool's Richie Rich then?"

"I dunno. Enough bread to bury the dead."

"His Jordans are tight as fuck." Kermit handed over the cash.

Trey shoved it into his jeans. "Dude's got a bunch at his house, he said."

"For real?"

"OGs, brand new—from '97. Not sure if I believe him though—" Trey heard the Suburban roar to life on the other side of the building. "Shit. Gotta roll."

"Nice doin' binness, cuz."

"First and last time, son. First an' last." Trey sprinted through the parking lot, hollering for everyone to wait up.

Kermit's father yelled for him outside the funeral home. He quickly opened the dumpster, slid the Smith & Wesson inside a sweaty McDonald's bag and stashed it before rushing back.

Isaiah was in his office, massaging the knot of his paisley tie back to its pristine form when his son rushed through the door.

"What is it, Dad?"

"Where were you?"

"Took out some garbage."

His stern look pierced the boy. "Need your help with deposits again."

"You know I can make them on your phone these days? I told you that, right?"

"Boy, *you* don't tell *me* shit. Why do I need to use a phone when I have you?"

Before Kermit could answer, the man brought up a fist. He winced.

"Such a weak, weak boy. Take after your bitch mother. But you already knew that—can feel the weakness coursing your veins, can't you?" He approached his desk and handed over Monty's check. "Take this to the bank *now*. The sum is too great to have lying around. They close soon."

Kermit's eyes bulged at the amount, just under eighteen thousand. Images conjured of a procession for Lil Meezy featuring a glittering hearse with twenty-four-inch spinning rims—or maybe Snoop playing the wake...His eyes fell on the check's signature. He scoped the top corner for the dude's details: *Montrose Laughlin, III, 210 16th Street, Manhattan Beach*—a palm struck the back of his head. "Fuh!"

Isaiah paused before a second blow. "Run along, boy."

Kermit pocketed the check and sped for his bicycle.

VI.

"No shit! You just...what—got a feather in your ass and decided to fly, huh?" Robbie reclined on Monty's couch, sipping White Sand IPA straight from a growler Monty had filled. "Paid for just the urn or the whole shebang?"

Monty leered out the windows, sunlight dancing about the tide. He licked froth from his upper lip, beer tasting better than any he'd ever had. Could feel Mother's disdain from the mantle, bellyaching his deed. "I ponied up for the whole tamale. Even tossed them a grand to handle the reception—food, booze, whatnot. They want me to go, but...I dunno."

"That's great, man. You *should* go. When Elle and I attend to these charity events, we don't ever get to see how much the donated funds accomplish firsthand—just read about it on a printout the following year—at the next event. You marched into ground zero and came out a hero. Better man, I can say that."

"Wanna come with? It'd blow their minds—a real Dodger in their midst."

Robbie paused to gulp. "When is it?"

"Tomorrow night."

"I'll see if I can move some stuff around."

"Prolly busy sitting on my other sofa, I suppose."

"What can I say? I'm a man of leisure these days. Plus, I hate the public seeing me in a sling like this—some fucking gimp."

"No one respects a gimp."

"So, tell me more about this family, man? The Craigs."

"Good people. Hard working. Father is an electrician—son, Trey, works for him."

"Hey, you should get them to finish wiring the outdoor security cameras. Might hook you up with a deal."

Monty thought about it, not caring about the expense. He did enjoy talking with the man and his son. Could be another chance to get to know them, outside of their family tragedy. After all, they were the first *real* folks he'd encountered in some time. "I should do that," escaped his lips, even though he knew deep down he probably wouldn't. After all, he'd just stepped out of his cocoon for a day, wasn't quite ready to welcome others inside just yet.

Kermit leaned his bicycle against a picnic table in Veterans Park, placing the McDonald's bag beside him as he sat atop warm wood. His stomach growled, having no time to grab a quick bite. A Rally's burger sounded nice. They told him to be here now but, obviously, the gun buyers weren't present. He hated having to deal with such thugs, but one had to do what they could to survive in these parts. His cousin, Young Mel, ran with this crew and vouched for Kermit. When Trey phoned with his proposition, Kermit dialed Mel soon as he clicked off the call. His stomach roared. As he doubled over, he locked onto his left hand, scribbled across the back of it in blue ink was the name and address on that check. *Montrose Laughlin III.* An idea had struck him as he waited inside the Wells Fargo, completing Father's errand. Maybe he could squeeze a few more bucks out of Mel's boys with it. Sell them the pistol, along with some information—the whereabouts of a rich fool giving away his wealth.

A dense mass of four bodies entered at the park's rear. As the blob came closer, its color set Kermit at ease, a legion of blue, puffing blunts, acting belligerent. He waved them over, as if he wasn't sticking out like a wart on a nose.

Mel came up close before smacking him upside the head. "The fuck you thinking, Kerm, carrying that piece in a goddam baggy. Hide the pistol on your person, fool. Don't be slippin'."

The other boys laughed, chiming in with their own taunts until Mel shushed them with the back of his palm. Kermit wanted to hand over the gun and run away that second, not being cut out for this type of thing. But then he'd be out all the money he'd saved working the past three months. And what the hell would he do with a gun? It'd be all for nothing. He humored the crew, acting as if he were just like them, swiping a hit from a blunt while one of the older boys inspected the merchandise. He'd have to act the part to get paid; couldn't let these jerks know how soft he actually was. An attack of coughs overcame him soon as he exhaled the plume. More laughter ensued. Someone called him a little bitch.

So much for saving face.

The older guy named Smoke purchased the pistol for three hundred, biting Kermit's profit to negative twenty-five dollars.

He lied and said he turned a dollar. For three hundred, the crew wanted to buy more, if he had any. Kermit poo-pooed the notion, claiming (like Trey had told him) that this was a one-time deal. He then proceeded to disclose his other item for sale.

"Hey, lookie here…"

He'd anticipated *some* interest when he told the crew about this rich dude in the South Bay, but their exuberant reactions took him by surprise, the boys all high as fuck, jonesing for a lick. When he said they could have the dude's address for another hundred, everyone roared in laughter. He pretended like he was playing too, nearly on his bicycle to head for a cheeseburger.

Mel pushed Kermit off the bike and forced him to come along, clawing the back of his neck, shoving him in the direction of a parked sedan. "You talk a big game, Kerm. Now take us to where this moneybags lives."

Without hesitation, Kermit surrendered the scribbles on his left hand.

The sun dipped its final brilliance through the living room windows as Monty and Robbie watched an Angels' game snoozer, tearing into the team's coach for not believing in sabermetrics, oblivious to the perfect L.A. sunset. A tirade out Robbie came to an unexpected halt.

Knocks at the door.

Monty glanced down at his phone before remembering the security monitor on the entrance wasn't hooked up; it had fed through his cell with a view of guests. Usually, it was either Robbie or UPS. He placed his pint down and went to a wall mount to buzz the person up. If it was UPS, they always left the parcel behind a front post. *Could be a neighbor signed for the package.* Monty craned to Robbie, now busy inspecting the nipples on the hallway bust; looked as if the growler was mixing perfectly with his pain meds. The elevator shaft began to whine. Robbie accompanied Monty in seeing who was here.

The doors began to part.

Elle Slate walked in wearing a soft red sundress, slightly buzzed enough to come over barefooted.

"Another cocktail party, Elle?"

She gave Monty a friendly embrace. "Got the gals headed over in a few."

Robbie: "What's up, babe?"

"The audio is messed up, a button got hit—haven't a clue."

Monty: "*Real Housewives* again?"

"*Bachelorette in Paradise.*"

Monty's eyebrows became enlightened.

Robbie pointed to the second growler on the counter. "I'm coming back, so don't kill that."

Monty opened the refrigerator for some pickles as the couple headed to the elevator.

Mel's Monte Carlo made it to Manhattan Beach just as the sun was gulped by the Pacific. He parked the sedan a few blocks from their target, having circled the block three times to scope the setting. Smoke loaded the pistol with six bullets from out Kermit's pocket. The crew got out, eyeing a sidewalk lined with manicured roses, cement clean enough to slurp spilled ice cream. They lit Newports in unison to brace nerves. Kermit pretended to smoke one, never inhaling, a trick he'd learned in middle school to avoid getting bullied. The five boys sat at a lone bus bench, trying not to turn heads. They tranced on the open ocean, its normal dark blue bleeding oranges and pinks. Was as if they'd only seen this type of thing in drugstore picture frames or a textbook from long ago. They waited for darkness to seep up the hill, bringing them back into their comfort zone. The moon sparked howls from backyard dogs. Mel punched Kermit's arm, signaling him to lead the way.

* * *

Monty had a clean buzz off his growler, closing one eye to focus on landing another pickle, spearing it with a knife. There were only a few left in this jar, all scurrying from his blade with each thrust as if they were alive, fish in a barrel, all smarter than him. He reclined on the sofa, exhausted from concentrating, belly full of red pepper, vinegar and dill. He checked the wall clock; there was no way he'd be able to stay awake if Robbie came back. These craft beers wore heavy on the brain. He'd had a full day too—one he was glad to have had but would most likely relive only once a year. Next time he'd do something nice on Christmas. He clicked off the television, steadying himself on seafaring legs. Approaching the counter, he emptied his pockets into a crystal candy dish, one Mother used for her beloved butterscotch. The checkbook sat prominent before a bowl of apples, stoic almost, as if it'd known what it accomplished today. Monty opened it to a carbon copy of *the* check, grin climbing his drunken face.

A stone tossed in a lake.

Ripples...all because of me.

He turned to Mother's urn, raised his fist and exploded the middle finger. *This is what* I *think about what* you *think, Mother.* He returned to the check, contemplating removing it from the pack to frame or laminate, maybe put above his toilet: a daily reminder of how great he could be...you know, when he felt like it. On second glance of the copy, a slight panic took hold.

The billing address.

He'd forgotten to buy new checks once moving into Mother's old house—*this* house. After years of extensive remodeling, he'd finally shifted all his things from next door, barely two years ago. Robbie became a Dodger around then, his people making an offer on the "Bastard Home" (Mother's words) that he couldn't refuse. How could he say no to a big leaguer...a potential celebrity friend? Oh, how embarrassing it would be if that check were to bounce. *Did things like billing address even matter these days?* He'd call the bank first thing tomorrow. *No need to worry the Craigs about it—not during this horrible time in their lives.*

Everything would be fine. He'd make sure of it. And order new checks. For next time.

"What. A. Doll. He did that?" Elle sipped Shiraz at the breakfast nook, watching Robbie eye the stereo system as if it were from Mars.

"Paid for everything. Cremation, urn. See, that's rewarding. No banquet. No autographs or selfies. Straight to the source." He punched the remote to zero response.

"It's them Vin Scully eyes, I tell ya. What a kind-hearted man."

"Don't remember what you pressed here, huh?"

"I didn't touch *anything*. Think Priscilla might've used it as a chew toy."

Robbie sent a dirty look at Elle's Yorkie, snoozing on the couch. "When's everyone supposed to be here again?"

"Soon. Like ten minutes."

"Fuck." He adjusted his sling, techno stress killing his buzz. A strange button at the top corner of the remote caught his eye. *Auto Vol?* He punched it and sound came blaring out the speakers. As he scrambled to save the subwoofer, Elle approached and draped an arm around him, planting a wet kiss, careful not to disturb his shoulder. Her breath was sour, pungent as bile. She began to undo his belt. "We have ten minutes..."

He slid his good hand up into her sundress, caressing the fold of her ass.

She went in for another hard kiss, but the doorbell stifled the moment.

Robbie cursed, redoing his belt. Elle went to freshen up for her guests. The second Robbie cracked the door's frame, he was met by a revolver pointed at his nose.

The computer screen lit up Trey's face in purple hues, his eyes scanning pages and pages of textbook sales, titles dancing in the glint of his eyeballs. Pops was asleep on his recliner; Mom busy putting the girls to bed. He scrolled a new page, eyeing a piece of paper with his undergrad curriculum requirements, then back at book titles. It was all happening, the future coming at him in spectral bursts. And all he had to do, so far, was numb his conscience. He sold a gun, so what? Who cared what others did with their own wretched lives? Not like he was pulling the trigger. He added another text to his online cart and thought, *I'd do plenty worse to this world just to be done with the neighborhood forever.*

Smoke held the gun steady as Young Mel had Kermit and the others use duct tape to bind the couple together on the floor. Hoods helped conceal all their faces. Kermit immediately knew something was wrong, too frightened to mention that he'd never seen this man (or woman) in the funeral home earlier. Didn't matter now. The act was in progress.

He was a full-blown criminal.

A safe in the bedroom had been opened by the husband; a quick smash to the face with Smoke's pistol helped speed the process. Dude's nose was gushing for days. Mascara exploded about the wife's eyes; her sobbing turned to gentle weeps. There weren't any Air Jordans like Kermit had promised; however, the guy had an unhealthy amount of Dodger gear. The three stacks out the safe softened that blow, just over thirty grand. Their shit dog began to yap at the door. Mel turned to see four older women, faces pumped to the max with Botox, all fisted with wine or champagne. The sight of Smoke's weapon sparked banshee screams, the ladies trembling in horror.

A bottle crashed to the ground.

Smoke jumped, accidently firing a round

Kermit ate the bullet, directly in the chest.

The boys scurried out a side door and sprinted up the block.

Kermit collapsed to the tile floor, eye to eye with the yapping dog, warm blood pooling beneath him until a coldness came over, one he'd only feel for the first time. *Such a weak, weak boy.*

Monty stirred from his drunken slumber, a pop followed by screams in the night disturbing sweet dreams. He got up to close the sliding glass door, gazing out at adjacent homes, not seeing anything alarming. *A car must've backfired, sparking someone's night terrors.* He climbed back into bed, feeling sorry for whoever was *that* frightened this time of night. He thought about his deed again and smiled, closing his eyes, licking his teeth. He'd place Mother's urn in a closet or drawer tomorrow. No need to have her so prominent within his house. *A truly great day, today.* The ocean purred him back to dreamland, an angel's sleep for the angel he was.

WHITE HORSE

Rain-soaked streets rarely happened in Hollywood, one of the perks of paradise. A man being chased could crouch into deep corners, fade into alleyways. Not tonight though. Ziggy had been sprinting for blocks. The circus of neon was relentless, shining up off the boulevards, exposing every pocket of sanctuary. He crouched behind a dumpster at the rear of Pink Elephant Liquor. Magenta beams from the store crept at his shoelaces. His eyeballs bugged. It was a Cutlass full of homeboys, from which gang, who knew? It didn't matter; he knew why they wanted him. Slanging dope was no longer ideal.

He waited for three cigarettes before heading back out, down Western. The streets were jammed with the usual Thursday night crowd, too many cars to keep track. He tucked his head and sped up, a horse with blinders. There was a lounge up ahead attached to a Super 8 motel. Place looked dark enough. An empty stool was out front. He ducked through the red curtain to get in off the streets.

The joint was cast in a crimson glow, damn near lethargic. A TV behind the bar spouted the Dodgers-Rockies game to an uninterested patron trapped in a Dean Koontz novel. He sidled up to the counter, taking a look around. The jukebox twisted CDs in silence, entertaining a lonesome pool table. Pictures of cheerful patrons cluttered every wall, slapping high fives, wagging tongues; an ironic twist. He drumrolled his palms on the wood to spark a bartender. The person reading put up a finger before dog-earing a page. An older woman, short hair. The moment the book shut, she became animated.

"Hey, darling, how are you?"

The exuberance caught him off guard. "Okay, I guess. Busy night, huh?"

"Later it will fill out." She smiled. "What you drinking?"

Her accent was foreign but he couldn't make it. Russian? Probably Armenian. "Bushmills-soda, please."

The pour was heavy. A splash of soda was music to his ears. She slid the tumbler his way, followed by two bowls of popcorn and almonds.

"Geez, what service."

She smiled, adjusting the volume on the TV. Her hand slapped her thigh. "Ugh. Can you believe this?"

He squinted to make out the score. Dodgers down two. "It's early, we'll pull it off."

She walked around the bar and took the first seat available. They watched Manny fly out. He figured her to be in her sixties, maybe a grandma. Her floral blouse screamed grandma.

"I'm Ziggy, by the way."

He stuck out his hand.

"Rosie." She shook it. "Ever been here before?"

He choked back a long pull and shook his head. "What's the place called?"

"The White Horse Inn—been here for twenty-seven years."

"Wow. Pretty impressive."

Just then, a skinny black man waddled into the place. He stood by the door as if lost. She excused herself and tended to him. Before she even got to him, he waddled back out the door. She peeked outside and rushed back.

"Ray, my bouncer, is supposed to be here already. He usually handles that."

"What, the homeless?"

"No, no. For some reason we get people in here thinking we

have girls to take upstairs into the rooms. I don't know how many times I have told people we don't do that here, but they just keep coming in. One of the bad things about being attached to the motel, I guess."

He laughed. "Well, don't worry about me, honey. I ain't Vice or nothin'."

She gave him a look as if he'd handed her an excellent report card. He killed the drink. She got up and poured another. Vin Scully shouted out the tube. Ethier hit a three-run homer. They cheered.

"Told ya," he said.

Their conversation continued. They talked books and sports. He listened about her athletic nephews. They had the jukebox rocking on shuffle, tons of Stones. She told him about how bad the area was. He acted surprised when she mentioned gangs.

"I'm serious," she said. "I held a shotgun on the roof to protect the place last summer, every night for a week. It was a turf war—at least that's what they say on the news."

"Yeah, I read about that in the *Times. Blood in the Streets.*"

She shrugged, "Boys will be boys, you know? Some of them come in here from time to time. You just treat them with respect and hope that they return the favor. That's really all you can do."

The Cutlass sat idling in a parking lot off Western, behind a janky adult bookstore. Four bald heads scanned from inside, green tattoos aplenty. The white wall tires and Daytons made the rust bucket look hard. Saddle blankets draping the interior hailed Mexico. They'd covered a lot of ground but knew the fucker was gone. Sneaky rode shotgun and tossed in an oldies mixtape. The Delfonics crooned. He turned to Chente, the driver. "Let's head back to the crib, *ese.*"

"What for? 'Bout to roust this fool in a minute. We're good."

Sneaky lasered a glare in response. He didn't need a reason to let up. He was in charge. Chente put the car in gear and creeped up the block. Sneaky dozed, hoping for two minutes of peace. His brain filled with various images of gourmet dishes: rack of lamb, éclairs, lobster tail, etc. He got stuck on a plate of seared ahi tuna with a wasabi/mint garnish, could almost taste it. This was his relaxation mode. Brain chef. He began to feel much better.

The pad was just south of Little Armenia; a twenties-built termite's dream with a wraparound concrete porch. Youngster was sitting on a couch out front, drinking a Mickey's grenade. He was white, unlike the rest. Maybe fifteen, wearing creased Dickies four sizes too big. His strawberry buzz cut made him look like a nectarine. He yelled at the guys as they approached the driveway. "Did you find him?"

Sneaky and Chente walked straight past the kid and into the house. No words. The other two sprawled on the porch with him after grabbing beers. They were twins, underweight with overbites. You could only tell them apart by their face tats, tears on opposite eyes. It took brazen acts to earn brands like that on the street, and they'd just gotten theirs before mobbing strip clubs legit. One of them spoke up.

"Nah. Found him where you said he was on Hollywood. *Joto* ran before we could get a bead on him, ay."

The kid fell back into the couch, shaking his head. "Shooot."

Sneaky and Chente sat in the dining room at a foldout poker table. Chente was the hood yes-man. Whatever needed to be done, they grabbed Chente. He was a big boy, six-two and thick as a refrigerator. Sneaky, not so much. His dirt 'stache begged for manhood but his bloodline made him a shot caller. His father was an OG, meaning he could aspire to nothing less. Chente could only dream of nothing more, acting as if Sneaky's Pops was his own. It had been this way for years, Sneaky always reminding Chente to be careful what he wished for.

They stared down at a yellow tablet with a list of names on it. People they had sold the bad shit to. They knew for sure that one guy had died already—Youngster's stepbrother, Jimmy. They should have tested every single baggy they bought. Half the shit was cut with more chemicals than coke. Small-time stuff. Never trust a *guero*. They'd been had.

Chente said, "What now?"

"Call around, see if anyone's seen this white boy rompin' the boulevard."

"Cool."

"Other than that, we just gotta wait. Fucker's making a killing selling that shit, ay. He'll turn up."

Whenever Sneaky acted hard like that it was exhausting but expected. He got up and approached a cracked mirror over the fireplace, brushing dandruff off his bald head, wondering what he'd look like with long black hair. His white T-shirt was stained at the collar. No biggie. He had a closet full of the plain janes. He hit the porch through a flimsy screen door that welcomed flies. The twins and Youngster sat silent, watching three kids across the street fight over a Big Wheel. He pulled out a joint and let her rip, trying to get back into character.

"Youngster."

The kid looked up. His eyes glazed over from the single malt grenade.

"Come in here. Lemme holla atchu for a minute."

As the kid rose, the bell of a late-night ice cream vendor rounded the corner. The twins jumped off the porch, scrounging their pockets. Youngster watched until Sneaky killed his excitement with, "Come on, fool."

He walked the kid through to the backyard. Chente was still on his cell, firing off Spanish. The yard was shaded from the moon by a monstrous tangerine tree. Rotten fruit filled the ground, omitting a potent scent of citrus better than a car freshener. He passed the kid the joint.

"Tell me how you met this *guero* again."

The kid fumbled at pinching the J before slobbering all over the butt. He exhaled nothing and said, "That Azteca mural—across from the Metro at Western and Hollywood. Dude approached me while I was smoking. Seemed pretty square. He floated me that sample I gave you."

"You didn't catch his name, right?"

"Nah, like I said."

Sneaky could see the kid was buzzing hard and let up. This was the third time grilling him on it today. "Okay, homie. I feel you. How was the funeral yesterday?"

"Shitty, man." His head kicked to the side. "The Moms is taking it hard, dog. That *gochina* of his didn't even show up either. *Puta.* I told him she was no good. Should've dumped her ass, right quick."

Sneaky rubbed the kid's fuzzy dome, trying to smooth out the first of many knocks. This lifestyle brought on more downs than ups. A merry-go-round of romanticized death; once you got on, you could never jump off. Sneaky knew it all too well but still occasionally dreamt of trying. He glared back at the kid, remembering what it was like bangin' at that age, trading awkward individuality for conformity and acceptance. Pure bullshit, he could only see that now. They used to call him Smiley back then. He tried hard to remember why. The kid peered up at him like a stray dog. "We'll grab this *joto, ese.* Don't even trip."

Ziggy was four drinks deep in no time, perfectly numb. The Dodgers' postgame show heralded the comeback victory. A pair of thirtysomethings in miniskirts marched through the curtain, letting in a sliver of moonlight. They were both brunette unless the red light was deceiving. The homelier one rushed over to Rosie and hugged her. Rosie's face looked like she'd bitten a lime. The other girl dipped her hand into his popcorn, chomping like it was dinner, sending him the eye.

"Oh, mama, I missed you," the hugger said.

Rosie feigned reciprocation.

They moved down to the far end of the bar, nearest the entrance. Rosie whipped up Cosmos. Upon closer examination, he could tell they didn't need the drinks. Their pupils were the size of Mickey Mouse ears. Rosie uncrumpled the twenty they handed her before shoving it into the register. She rolled her eyes, perching back onto her stool.

She whispered, "They aren't supposed to be in here. The one that hugged me, Carly, got eighty-sixed last night. I don't know the other one. What good's a bouncer when he doesn't show up, huh?"

"You want me to tell them to leave?"

"No, darling. It's fine. She doesn't remember."

They blatantly stared at the girls, skyrocketing through their weird world of narcotic bliss. He tried to share her disgust but gazed on at potential clients.

"Poor thing," she said, "I can't believe she's back in here again. Her boyfriend just died a few days ago."

He turned to her with a scrunched brow. She got up and approached a far wall, tearing a pair of pictures from it. She handed them to him. Carly was in both, sidled next to a clean-cut, polo-shirt type. Looked like a nice enough guy. He wondered why he was settling for *her*. Carly's face was a billboard for hard times and worse decisions.

"What happened?"

"Overdose. So shameful. I warned him so many times."

He glanced back at the girl carrying on at the end of the bar as if life were peachy. She had to be on a bender. He could probably unload the rest of his stash. Rosie delved back into her book. He stood and fingered the packets in his pocket before heading for the men's room.

A single light flickered above the toilet. He was sure to lock the door before seeing exactly what he had left. Two green baggies the size of matchbooks. The diamond emblem on each let him know they were already cut, way beyond ribbons. He'd give them both to the girls for fifty bucks. A steal. For him at least. Unload it and bail, he thought, exiting without a flush.

Sauntering over to the jukebox, he asked if anyone had any

requests. Rosie said, "No." He turned his attention to the girls. This was his usual approach. The bait: innocently invite them into your world. Carly stopped from sipping her Cosmo. She wanted to hear some Rancid. He could've guessed that.

"Shit, that's my favorite band of all time, girl. You got good taste."

She could've picked any band—Stryper, for fuck's sake. Didn't matter, he'd love them just the same. They exchanged smiles. She was nibbling at the hook. He grabbed a seat by them; close, but not too close. There was a brief introduction, customary, dull. The other girl was Tanya. The girls picked up where they'd left off, before he moved in, talking about some cunt named Mallory. Bitch had the "pampalomer virus" or something. Too much time on her back.

Tanya went on and on, gnashing in between words like a cow at pasture. "So, this bitch has the audacity to sleep with my ex-husband and get this...he left me for her."

"No," Carly gasped. Her pupils nullified shock.

The two interacted as if just getting acquainted. Ziggy sat limp as whiskey dick, waiting for an *in* on the conversation. Rosie was back to book worming. The juke wanted *Salvation*. Carly was blindsided by the tune.

Come on baby, won't you show me what you got...

"Man, I remember when I heard this for the first time," she told Tanya.

The *in*. He blurted, "Where were you?"

"A parking lot at Rat Beach. Me and my girls were partying with peppermint schnapps. Saw berries and made a run for the lifeguard tower. My first time busted by the cops. Prolly should've lowered the stereo, I guess."

"Beach bunny, huh?"

"South Bay girl." She let out a party *whoop-whoop*.

He improvised. "Shit, I knew a chick from down that way." He thought of a wholesome suburban name. "Stephanie? Stacey?"

Tanya got up to use the ladies' room. Carly scooted closer.
"What high school did she go to?"

"Uh, I really don't know—she was big into coke, I know
that."

She scoffed, "Who isn't?"

He leaned over close to her ear. She reeked of lilac. He
whispered those magic words. "I'm holding." Her eyebrows
jumped with bona fide interest—hook, line and sinker.

Youngster napped in the living room once the world stopped
spinning. None of Chente's phone calls had panned out but
now all the homeboys were on white boy lookout. The twins
were still out front, puffing blunts, eagerly into a blistered game of
bloody knuckles. Sneaky lounged in the back bedroom, studying a
recipe from a Mario Batali cookbook he found at the Goodwill.
Sausage cacciatore. He often imagined being a world-class chef,
working in Paris or Vegas with one of those funny hats. In this
life, his best dish was a mean peanut butter molé. Cooking was
relaxing for him, peaceful. That's what he planned on doing in
the next life.

Dodger highlights lit up the television as Chente poured every
bad gram they had left from the *guero* into a salad bowl on the
kitchen table. Tiny green baggies with diamonds speckled the
floor. A large metal sauce spoon was gonna help him cook every
last drop.

"Sneaky, grab me the rig back there," he hollered. "The big
one, ay."

Sneaky approached from the far room, holding a black
leather pouch, bound by a rubber band. He handed it to
Chente, busy refilling a butane lighter the shape of a pistol.

"Why you using my sauce spoon, dog?"

Chente rolled his eyes. "Don't worry. I ain't gonna ruin it."
He snapped off the band and opened the pouch on the table.
The needle inside was one he ganked from the hospital last time

he broke his hand on some knucklehead's melon. He saw a doctor plunging cortisone into a chick's shoulder with one just like it. He managed to grab three freshies but this was the only one he had left. The syringe looked like an empty baby bottle.

The kid woke up and saw them. "Whatcha two doin', man?" Chente said, "Making a hot shot."

Youngster watched as the rig sucked up a gooping spoonful. "You're fuckin' crazy if you slam that, ay."

Chente chuckled, scooping another spoonful and adding water droplets. "I ain't stoopid, fool." The pistol torched. "This hot shot is for *our* hot shot, ay—when we find his ass. I want you to see the look on his face when his heart explodes."

The machismo in the air hurt Sneaky's brain.

All five of them were huddled around the table now, watching as Chente finalized the vile with disaster fluid. The twins said the juice looked like warm menudo. A rustling came from upstairs. Youngster and the twins hit the porch. They knew what was up there, about to come down; Sneaky's father. Chente and Sneaky remained at the table. A nervous twitch was on both their faces as footsteps thumped down the stairway. A hulking menace of a man yawned behind them. His face half covered by a thick, overgrown mustache. He was fifty-ish with a stone chest and arms, blurred ink in abundance. Anyone could see he had a few stints under the belt. He went straight for Sneaky, slapping him on the back of the head as if it were a stripper's ass.

"Why ain't you wake me up, fool? Supposed to be at work coupla hours ago, motherfucker."

Sneaky rubbed the back of his bald dome. "Sorry, Pops. We found that *joto* who burned us and chased him in the Olds."

Chente rose and embraced Ray with their signature handshake and a half hug, fists bopping each other's back.

"You chop him down or what, Chente?"

"Nah, Ray. Fucker busted a Carl Lewis."

"Shit." Ray laughed and looked at Sneaky. "Buncha small timers, ay." His eyes caught the syringe on the table. "The fuck?"

Chente rushed to it and said, "I thought of this, Ray—for the *guero*, when he peeks his head. Word's out on the streets already. Dead man walking, ay."

"*Odelay, mijo.*"

Sneaky marveled at what life had dealt him as a father, the back of his head still tingly with pain. Ray hadn't called him *mijo* in forever. His mind drifted back to Batali's cacciatore medley, wondering if it was a family recipe.

The big man walked over to the rotary phone in the kitchen. "Gotta call work 'cause a you two *vatos*. Rosie's gonna be fuckin' pissed."

The phone rang twice before she answered. "White Horse Inn."

"Rosie. It's Ray."

"Where the heck are you, darling? I'm all by myself here."

"Fell asleep. Sorry. I'll be there in a few. Is it busy?"

"No." She whispered. "That girl's back though—Carly. She's with a new girl. Saw them buying something off this white kid a minute ago—little green bags. He didn't seem like trouble at first. Got to be drugs, right? You need to kick them all out."

"Shit. Alright, mama. I'm on my way."

The phone hit the receiver, and he hurried to grab his SECURITY windbreaker. "Chente, drop me off at the White Horse." He caught wind of the baggies strewn at Sneaky's feet. He pointed. "Those the baggies the white boy sold you?"

Sneaky said, "Yup."

"I think this fucker's slangin' at the lounge right now, ay. Rosie said that bitch Carly hit up some fool—green baggies."

The boys outside heard everything and stood alert. Chente had the car keys in hand and pounced out the door. Ray got back on the phone and told Rosie what was up. She obliged to stall the *guero* if he tried to leave. Sneaky made for the door until Ray noticed the syringe, still lying on the table. "Grab that shit, stoopid!" Sneaky flinched. He ran back, picked up the rig and made for the Cutlass.

* * *

The trio was getting sloppy at the end of the bar, launched by liquor and whatnot into that perfect void. Rosie hung up the phone and stared on, wondering if this really was the prick responsible for Jimmy's OD. If so, what a cruel world, allowing Carly to be seated at his hip, basking in sweet ignorance. She got up and poured them a stiff complimentary round. Ziggy shot up his hands in protest.

"Whoa, Rosie. I think it's past my bedtime. I really should be getting on."

Carly and Tanya pawed at his denim jacket in protest. He'd let them test plenty of his personal stash, the good shit, before unloading the bad. They were his now. He was the man of the hour but for all the wrong reasons. In a blink, he pictured the many things he could get the girls to do for him, to him, to each other. Rosie broke his carnal reverie.

"Nonsense, darling. Just one more—on the house. I'll whip up a hot dog for you, too. Don't want you out there with an empty stomach."

Carly said, "She really does make a mighty good hot dog, Zig."

Tanya wet her lips. "I just love a good foot long."

His ass hit the cushion, pronto. One more drink would do. Looked like the plan just got sidetracked. The party flowing in his bloodstream was working overtime. He took a long pull off the fresh tumbler. Why did he come in here again?

The dogs were as good as any microwave could muster. The girls' eyes nagged him for more bumps in the bathroom. Rosie pointed a digital camera at them from across the bar. "Say cheese." The three of them barely showed teeth before she snapped the shot. "For the wall," she said.

Carly whispered in his ear, "Tanya's got a room for tonight."

110

Her eyes went to the ceiling. "You should come up for a while."
He tried not to get flush. "Okay," he said. "I'll hang for a few."

The girls got animated, clawing at their purses, trying to stand up straight. Rosie overheard them and tried to sling three more hot dogs. Ray would be there any minute. It was too late. The trio pounced out the front curtain, saying goodbye with a single wave. She picked up the phone and dialed.

"Super 8. Monica speaking."

"Hi, Monica. This is Rosie. I need a favor, darling. Three people are about to walk in, one of the girls has a room for the night. Call me back and let me know which number, okay?"

"Sure thing, mama."

The Cutlass pulled into the White Horse's adjacent parking lot. Youngster was stuffed in the trunk since the cab was jam-packed. There were at least five Glocks in there with him, poking at his back. When the lid opened, the first thing he saw was Ray's chiseled arms, yanking him out like a sack of potatoes.

The twins surveyed the lot for bystanders. They didn't want to take out guns while people were watching. Ray led the way after the boys suited up, grabbing a roll of duct tape before slamming the trunk. They swooped into the lounge, expecting the best. Instead of meeting the *guero* eye to eye, they stood watching Rosie, reading a book. She put up her finger, dog-eared a page and pulled out the camera.

"This the guy, Ray?"

He grabbed it and showed the picture to Youngster.

"That's the motherfucker, *ese*." He double checked the photo and noticed his brother's girlfriend on the guy's left. He couldn't believe it. *Puta.*

Ray said, "Where'd he go?"

Rosie stepped behind the bar and grabbed a shotgun from below. She placed it on the counter. "Upstairs. Room 208."

Ray almost handed the shotgun to Sneaky before rethinking and tossing it to Chente instead. The rest of the gang sped out the door. He hung up his bouncer jacket on the coat rack near the entrance and followed. Rosie could hear the thudding pitter-patter as the boys rushed up in the motel to the second level.

Carly and Tanya were sprawled across the seashell bedspread, mouth to mouth, tongues wrestling, clothes gently coming off thanks to each others' grimy claws. They giggled and moaned for Ziggy to come play. He was sitting on the toilet with the bathroom door locked. Who would've thought a threesome could be so daunting? Seemed like the party was everywhere but his cock. He sat there in a towel, thinking happy thoughts, trying to beat life into it.

There was a hard thud at the door. The girls yelped. He stood, opened the bathroom door, "Who's there?" The girls were locked in embrace at the foot of the bed. Brown and pink areolas, cookie to cookie. They were as alarmed as he was. A second thud. A third. Before he could get his pants on, the door cracked open at the hinges and six armed men flooded the room. There was a shotgun to his nose before he could get a look at their faces. He didn't have to. Their bald heads said plenty.

The twins man-handled the girls, grabbing them by the hair and slapping till quiet. Ray secured the door, making sure no tourists on the floor got nosey while Chente and Youngster confronted the *guero*, bawling like a baby.

Youngster said, "Remember me, fool?"

Ziggy's eyes popped.

Chente said, "Fuck yeah, he does."

Ray tossed the duct tape to the twins. Chente kept the shotgun leveled as they neutralized the trio, smothering their mouths with sticky strands.

The girls were hog-tied and put in the bathtub. Youngster belted Carly with his tiny fist, cracking the bridge of her nose.

She became a faucet, weeping as he berated her for missing Jimmy's funeral. He tore off the gag and asked about the picture on Rosie's camera, implying she helped the *guero* kill his stepbrother. She pleaded ignorance, told how they just met. He didn't care, smacking her again and again. It just felt right.

Ziggy was strapped to a lone desk chair, watching in horror as Chente flicked bubbles from inside a monster syringe. Sneaky sat on the bed, spacing out into nowhere, cradling his gun. This caught Ray's attention.

"Chente, give that shit to Sneaky. I wanna see him do it."

"I got it, Ray. Ain't no thang, *ese.*"

Ray's silence spoke volumes.

Chente let out a disgruntled sigh before nodding in compliance. Ray's eyes got huge as Sneaky rose slowly toward Chente's outstretched arm.

"Don't be a pussy," said Ray. "Gotta start actin' like a real man sometime, homie."

Sneaky never knew what the hell that meant. He'd been hearing it his whole life from Ray, the months he was out of the clink—a *real* man. He snatched the rig from Chente's grip.

Chente used the white boy's belt to tie off a tourniquet. Sneaky's hand trembled, buzzing the syringe over a bulbous vein. He squinched his eyes. The giant needle attacked Ziggy's arm like a prehistoric mosquito. He thrashed to no avail. Snot flew from his nostrils. The moment Sneaky hit the vein, Chente yelled for Youngster.

The kid came from the bathroom and saw what was about to go down.

"Come here," Chente said. "I want you to look this fool in the eyes and tell him what's up."

Ziggy's eyes were swimming from the tiny amount of poison already trickling through his arm.

Youngster said, "This is for my brother, Jimmy. He died snorting your shit, *joto.*"

For a split second, Ziggy almost knew what the kid was

talking about.

Ray yelled, "Do it already."

Sneaky began to plunge the rig and then stopped, frozen, trembling.

Chente uttered, "What the fuck?"

Sneaky's heart pumped crazy. He could hear Ray approaching and anticipated the smack. He closed his eyes. *Mario Batali. Sausage cacciatore.* His head jarred to the left, his ear on fire. *Seared ahi tuna. Wasabi/mint garnish.* Ray grabbed Sneaky's hand, forcing it on the plunger, all the way down. *Mario Batali. Sausage cacciatore.*

All six of them watched on as the *guero* convulsed and foamed, his insides about to blow, eyes frozen at Youngster. The kid would see those eyes forever, he knew it instantly. Nightmares.

Ray was pissed. "Do something with these girls, *vatos*. I'm going back to work."

Chente turned to Sneaky, trying not to laugh. "Let's turn them out for a few bucks in downtown, ay."

Sneaky nodded, spinning around to see Ray shaking his head out the door in disgust. He pulled out the rig, stared at the dead white boy and prayed to swap souls with the bastard.

Ray grabbed his SECURITY jacket and pulled the stool in from out front. He posted up near the entrance, on duty. An older gentleman with silver hair approached. Ray acknowledged him with a nod. The old guy mumbled something about girls being available inside. Ray said, "We don't do that shit here anymore, gramps. How many times I gotta tell you, fools? Get the fuck on, already."

The man looked startled, shuffling back to his eggshell Deville.

Rosie could hear the boys fumbling around upstairs. She looked up from her book at the ceiling, then back at Ray. He shrugged his shoulders. She didn't ask. She already knew.

"You want a hot dog, darling?"

"Sure, mama. Make it two."

FULL BLOOM

She scratched at black gravel bits embedded in her palm, cursing that dumb sonofabitch in whispers, first one she'd laughed with in months, danced for, cared some, came damn close to loving, but weren't they all like that? Two press-ons splintered before removing a single pebble. She sucked the digits, pausing for pain in the middle of the boulevard. A Datsun swerved around, horn whimpering, straining to clutch its lawnmower in the bed. Her head pounded. *Could be worse.* The roll had saved her. Luckily, when kicked out a car, practice makes perfect.

Daybreak teased as she smacked along, barefoot. The casualties of an all-nighter were strewn about a porch couch up ahead: two boys, hairless, slender, college. Music seeped out the windows and brought goose bumps. She adjusted her pleather halter, wishing for a compact to spruce up. Purse was probably flung from the Porsche too. She winked at the boys before marching inside their apartment.

Slanted posters rehashed her teenage music catalogue, verbatim: Descendents, Circle Jerks, Op Ivy. Those vibrant days; the world in front of her. A shirtless blonde was slunk on a stool, over a tallboy. She went for the fridge and got her own, its door plastered with band stickers. The High Life went down smooth. She searched tabletops for good time paraphernalia, fiending for anything but this. Footsteps came from the hallway. She stood erect, amplifying her assets. A fat longhair emerged, eyes bugged.

"Who the fuck are you?"

She giggled. "Hey there."

The guy's head gave a Labrador tilt.

"Got Tina?"

"Tina who?"

"No, silly." She plugged a nostril. "*Tina*—got any?" She approached, strumming his chest through an open vest.

"Ugh, Chip might—where'd you come from?"

"Your dreams, honey. Which one's Chip?"

He awoke the slumping blonde, filling him in before grabbing the others out on the porch. Chip staggered to life, pounding dregs before holding her close. His neck pulsed praying hands.

"Whatchu gonna give me for it, huh, princess?"

She turned her head from his sour mouth, effortlessly removing her top. The act struck paralysis in the boys walking in. Her hands honked and smooshed.

"Just gimme some—see what happens."

Haggard eyes met across the room. One of the couch crew mouthed, *Whoa*. The other whispered, "Dude, she's like forty."

Chip rifled through his pockets, dangling a baggie before her giant eyes. "Mitch, call Germ to bring more over."

She grabbed the dope and pressed it to her heart. The fatty swooped keys off the table, handing them over as Chip fumbled with her rhinestone belt buckle. Scooping a monster bump, she fixated on the keychain, a Walk of Fame star—some girl's name on it. She reminisced for a beat, licking her lips before blasting into normalcy.

"Holy shit—Lucille Ball!"

A slovenly black woman rolled her eyes under tents of purple eye shadow. "That's nice, baby. Come on."

"Sorry. Never saw these stars before."

"You gonna have plenty a time, balee dat. First time in Cali?"

"Nah—from Torrance."

The woman flinched. "And you've *never* seen these?"

"Nope. Never ventured out...'til now, I mean."

"How old a you?"

"Older'n I look."

"Sure you wanna do this?"

"Yeah, why not?" Slumming for change on Melrose wasn't exactly panning out.

"'Kay, most nights you just be hangin' at that D.T. on Santa Monica. Saturday's doh, you be here—appointments only. I'll grab da room fo' ya but don't want none a dem fools you run wit makin' it a shootin' gallery, ya hear?"

She nodded. "I don't do that stuff, you know?"

"Don't give a fuck, sista. Ya binness, ya binness—long as it don't fuck wit *my* binness. On dat note." The girl rifled through her clutch, pulling out a glass rose and torch. "Let's roll back a sec."

They ducked from blinking neon into an alley, huddling behind a rusted dumpster. Startled cockroaches scurried for sanctum as her new friend twirled the rose at her lips, crackling its contents into a thin grey plume. Her turn. Once the goods were gone, they lit Newports and wandered back under the electric circus.

"'Kay, girl. You meetin' da first one on Selma an' Wilcox. Here."

Eyes drooping, she grabbed the key outstretched to her.

"Need me to go over da rates again?"

"No—no. I got it. Money first."

"You be fine."

She smiled. "Thanks, Charmaine."

"Call me Mama, girl."

"Momma?"

"Ya-huh, dats what they all be callin' me. Whateva you need, just ask Mama."

She began to tear, looping arms around those gargantuan

hips, ear nestled on those giant pillows. Gentle beats of the heart were soothing. The party in her brain helped too. Could stay like this forever.

"Shh—shh. Mama's here, baby. Gonna be awright. You safe now."

The rafters shook once her back slammed into the wall, droplets of holy water raining upon her like a firestorm on innocent civilians. She thrashed to no avail. A dining room chandelier flickered at random. Her mother's grip was too strong, too righteous, slamming her repeatedly into the light switch while praising his name with conviction.

"Save her, Lord! My baby girl is lost! Show her your light and goodness, oh King of Kings!"

She spat at the woman's mouth, managing to break free once the recoil, sprinting for refuge in the living room.

"Forgive her, Lord! She knows not the evil of her transgressions!"

She lunged for the fireplace, grabbing a poker, wishing it was red hot. Her face was soaked, salvation fire now bombing at a distance. Mother stood before the shaking lance at her guts, eyes closed, mumbling scripture while raising a jazz hand.

"Stay back! I'll fucking kill you."

An eerie calmness made its way through the homely woman's core. Long, smooth inhales brought her back down from heaven. "Darling, the Lord has a plan for you and it's not this—let him guide you. Be one with the Spirit."

"I said stay back!" *Fuck your god, Mother.* "I'm leaving for good."

The woman smiled, whispering, "Forgive her Jesus," before the rage. "How in the heck do you think you're gonna make it out there—you're only a child."

"I'll be eighteen in a week, Mother. Now, step aside."

"Honey, you are going to the cleansing retreat—Pastor Tim

already set everything up. We can't go disappointing the church's wishes now."

Hypocrite. "Mother, how many times do I have to say it? This is *your* church. I've respected that and kept my mouth shut when you made the decision, but since you've been saved..."

"Honey...why can't it be *our* church? You know He loves you—you were made in His likeness."

The floating smile was a dagger.

"Mother..." She began to sob, poker going lax.

"Here—here. Come into these arms."

"No!" The iron shot up to her throat.

The woman held her ground, raining more salvation, praising for His guidance.

She felt the cool of the window at her back. With Mother's eyes closed, she swung, shattering it with two blows. Never felt such strength. The woman lunged but years of weight had her slow. She went through the hole like a rabbit from hound, then running, running, till the burning quashed inside.

Their creepers pounded pavement; hers plaid, Cat's cheetah. Cat grabbed the sixer without even telling her. Actually, she did yell, "Run." An immigrant clerk shook his fist under amber fluorescence. His stature diminished with each pounce into darkness. After four blocks, they took sanctuary on some church steps, struggling for air between giant bursts of laughter.

"You...fuckin'...bitch."

Cat gave a sly grin. "Oh...I know you love me. Break out those smokes."

She reached in her denim vest, black patches Frankensteined askew. "Barely had 'em in my hand before you bailed. We need a better system."

"Nah," cracking an Icehouse, "just better beers."

She lit two cigs and handed one over.

Cat exchanged it for a can, taking a puff. "What the hell

are these?"

She held the stick away from her face and read the pack. "Benson & Hedges. Menthol?"

"Fuck, we do need a better system."

She seeped smoke, ignoring the inhale. "What time the show start?"

"Last time they played Frogs, doors opened at eight."

"Twenty-one and over, right?"

"Fuck yeah—ganked my sister's ID. Got one, right?"

"Yup, looks nothin' like me either."

"Whatever, man. Know it'll work."

She swilled skunk. "Gross. Wish you'd grabbed cold ones for a change."

"I fuckin' got what I could, bitch. You're on the brew crew tomorrow."

They forced more gulps.

"I like that new color."

Cat strummed purple locks pouring from her temples; head was shaved everywhere else. "Thanks."

"Wish I could do mine like...like slime green."

"Do it."

She slurped and shrugged.

"Who gives a shit about your mom? Just do it."

"I know—it's just...I dunno."

"You only get one life, bitch. Do what the fuck you want."

"I'm tryin'."

"Yeah, yeah. Banzai!"

They both chugged their cans, piss liquid dribbling off their pimples.

Cat burped, "Winner."

She grabbed her stomach, willing the liquid to stay down. "Big surprise."

"Oh, shit. Check out what else I got from my sister's drawer."

They stared at a Ziploc harboring grey, earthy shreds.

"What is it?"

"You never done 'shrooms before?"

She grimaced. "You have?"

"No but...come on, we'll each take a handful. It's prolly just like that tree we smoked at Ronnie's. How could it be worse?"

"Ugh..."

"Come on, you know it'll be sick. Need something to get you on that stage."

"Oh, man. If I get up there, Milo's gettin' the wettest kiss ever."

They chuckled, pausing in blank stares.

"Don't be such a pussy."

She watched as Cat pretended they didn't taste like turds. The baggy landed on her lap. Thoughts of her mom driving up were sent to the back of her brain. Like the woman was even capable; she'd never leave Craig at that pub all by himself. She flicked the cig and proceeded to munch.

She wiggled toes in the warm sand, lapping dollops of mayo from the corners of a crustless baloney sandwich. Salt in the air made it twice as good. Her father's thick fingers swabbed breadcrumbs off her cheeks, wiping them on his navy button up, a cursive *Rick* stitched over his heart. She turned to spot Mommy, smoking in the distance. They ate in silence, watching silken waves crash as surfers paddled for glory.

"You know this has nothing to do with you."

She squinted up at him.

"It's just one of those things that sometimes happen to grown-ups." He paused for a bite.

"Where are you going, Daddy?"

"Honey, I'm not going anywhere. Who said that?"

She glanced over her shoulder again. Mommy's back was turned.

He mumbled, "Fucking Christ."

At the shore, children retreated from icy whitewash, screaming till the tides sucked it all back in. One of the kids, a girl about her age, didn't make it, knocked over by a gentle wave as her friends laughed with their whole bodies.

"Listen, don't believe everything your mother tells you, okay?" She squinted back up.

"There's gonna be a lot of things said about me and none of it's true. Your mother's no angel either..."

Her sandwich dropped to the sand.

"Uh-oh." He snatched it up, handing her the remainder of his. "Here you go, princess."

She smiled, carefully cropping the edges, palms encrusted by granules. Mommy's voice resonated behind.

"So, did you tell her?"

Daddy rose, clapping sand from his tush. "No, I haven't—think it should be her choice, Donna. At least ask her what she wants—I mean, look where the fuck our decisions have brought us."

A whistle blew from the lifeguard tower. She watched as a leathery man grabbed a rescue buoy and sprinted to the shore. A woman bounced in a frilled one-piece, finger out, howling at the sea as the lifeguard dove with precision.

Her parents bickered as she approached the commotion. Children and surfers peered with porcelain eyes as the lifeguard waded through riptide, clutching a limp body to his chest; the girl beaten by the wave. A yellow patrol truck approached with caution, orange berries twirling atop. More guards helped splay the girl on a stretcher before attempting resuscitation. She gazed on in wonder till being pulled up by Mommy and whisked away.

"Rick, I gave you chance after chance and you fucked 'em all up. We'll just settle this in court, okay?"

Daddy pleaded as she nestled her ear to Mommy's fluttering heartbeat. Morbid images flourished for the first time; this cruel, cruel world. She pretended it was fake, all of it. That little girl was still running from those waves, screaming under the sun, basking in the confines of an unforgettable day.

* * *

Donna vacuumed the breeze through her nostrils, exhaling slowly out the mouth: in, out, repeat. Her nerves were a sparking livewire; tears beaten back by fits of laughter. Dread, fear, shame and angst pinballed through her core. Shouldn't she be happy with such news? Strumming her navel in gentle circles, she strode down PCH with purpose.

Pierside Liquor was the first stop. Best way to track his scent. Wayne was on shift, reloading Chesterfields above the register. Bottles behind him bounced soft beams of dusk. He paused at her rapid approach.

"You seen Rick?"

"Earlier. Was headin' down to the Bull Pen."

"What he buy?"

"Nothin' really—smokes and a scratcher."

"He comes back, tellim I gotta talk to him."

"Sure thing."

The Bull Pen was a good mile plus. Why didn't she change out of these damn flip-flops? Not like she hadn't made the same trek in them before. Rick was a rambler, one of the many strange tics that reeled her in. That smile too—whenever up to no good. Those tiny fucking teeth.

Darkness cast heavy in the bar, broken by the glow of a heated Dodgers-Angels skirmish. A short barkeep diced lemons before an elderly couple, squabbling over the exact location of Desilu Studios.

"Hey, Donna. The usual?"

"I'm good, Marty. Seen Rick today?"

He nodded. "Stopped by for a few. Left coupla hours ago."

"Say where he's headin'?"

He shrugged. "Oh, wait. Mentioned something about The Deuce."

She grumbled a "Thanks."

Even with the sun at its lowest point, she shielded her eyes out the door. The Deuce was only a few blocks back. What she wouldn't give for that drink. Her mind juggled names of girls to kill the craving. Shasta—too trashy. Marcy—that bitch from kindergarten. Blisters burned on each hammer toe, heels pink and calloused. Better be there.

She marched down the back corridor toward bursts of laughter. Sounded like the usuals in attendance: pier rats, avenue locals, high school ex-boyfriends. Was dead on except for some newcomers gracing corner stools: two blondes, twenties, bush pigs. The men were huddled, loopy, being boys. Place smelled like kid hair. She shot an awkward eye, yuks puttering as she approached. Clanks from the shuffleboard broke the silence.

"Tommy, where's Rick?"

An overweight postman raised his shoulders before diving back into his glass.

"Spuds?"

A lanky burnout turned to the rest of the pack.

Her hands shot out. "Anybody?"

One of the girls let out a squeal.

"The fuck's this cunt laughing at?"

The girls giggled in unison, and then she heard it, coming from the men's shitter. She paused at the door, knowing damn well the sounds bellowing inside. Her palm pressed it open. Rick's back and bare ass. Some redhead, legs pretzeled around, red nails clawing.

"Shut the fuckin' door, Spuds."

She pulled back slowly before gunning past stone patrons and out the front door.

Commuters whizzed reckless down the boulevard as she tranced at their taillights, stomping toward home—*their* home. She kicked off the flops and braved on barefoot. Forced fits of laughter fell short; the battle lost this time. Rustling palm fronds kept her company. She commenced juggling names. Then it hit. *Joy*—if it was indeed a girl. A smile came under glistening cheekbones. Look out world, Joy was coming to conquer.

THAT DREADED UNDERTOW

The best is when moonlight hits their scales just so, squirmy little bastards trying to avoid the inevitable: a giant hook through the gills. I work twilight because Marty pays us a little more. Free soda and liverwurst sammies too. Denny got me the gig, a favor he pulled after the Sport King kicked us off their half days. Some Japanese dude pulled a sculpin overboard and dangled it before three Boy Scouts' noses. Must've thought its fiery spine wasn't dangerous. All I did was grab the kids—shoved them toward a bait tank.

Denny cut the line and tossed the fish back home. Shouldn't have called the guy that harsh slur or flashed the blade to his cheek but Denny is Denny. Been the same way since high school. Preschool. Hell, around here, nobody ever changes.

I've seen the Pacific at its angriest. Choppy—foamy as grandma's spittle. Tonight she has her moments. Too rough to drop anchor, Denny captains the vessel through white caps. Everyone clings in the galley and makes each other sick. You deal with the barf. Tourists—a few regulars, even. Hosing down their dinner gives me time to reflect on all that's swimming beneath. Giant majestic creatures whose lives make mine feel like a big joke. Adventurers gliding through salt and brine, never ever trapped in one place. Lucky devils in their killer abyss.

Denny calls me a faggot to lighten the mood for everyone. I

shake it off like nothing, squirting vomit off the deck, contemplating wonders of the deep. Blue-faced "fishermen" point and laugh at me. Another night lost beneath the stars.

We head to a walk-up grease pit on the pier called Charlie's every dawn after pulling in and carving fillets from the night's catch. Two-dollar beers and decent nachos make breakfast. Other deckhands and captains crowd around four plastic tables, playing cards and yelling at one another. Denny and I grew up with every single one of them in some way: knew their brothers or sisters, friends of our fathers. Redondo Beach, Los Angeles County. You can have it.

I lean on the same corner nook, eat my nachos and sip two Bud Lights. Every morning, a self-imposed two-beer limit. Denny sucks them down like Cactus Cooler and slaps backs, grinning, rehashing youth. Stories we've all lived but forgotten. There's something great about hearing them over and over—rager parties, epic surf, beach bunnies we'd all taken for a ride. Barely forty with that golden window at our backs. What else was there to do?

The pier looks beautiful this morning, but I'd be a fool to mention it. Might as well talk about the current book I'm reading. No. Denny is on a tear, blasting any fool with an opinion. Even the seagulls are chuckling.

Main reason we all come to Charlie's is because of Rusty. Well, I come for my two-beer breakfast (which I pay for), but everyone else relies on Rusty. He's an old boozer who sits at a bench near the spinning pretzels. Never says a word. His ongoing tab is what sparks popularity. Most of these fiends couldn't even cop a buzz if it weren't for old Rusty. Hell, we don't know shit about the guy other than his pockets run deep as the...listen, the guy's loaded. I mean, you couldn't tell from the soiled jacket and filthy beard but it's true. He could be Elvis or Hoffa, but nobody ever bothers to find out. I introduced myself once but he wouldn't even look me in the eye. I won't let a man spot me a drink if he can't look me in the eye. Try to be my own man anyway—you can keep your handouts, Rusty. Everyone else doesn't dare rock the boat...so to speak.

I usually wait until Denny is at least four beers deep and goes to take a leak before I split. Today he must be super dehydrated as he sucks the head off cup number six. This greenhorn, Carl, is telling everyone how bad a surfer his brother is. Soon as he finishes, I know what's coming, so I gulp the ass-end of my beer and begin to shake hands. Almost make it out, but Denny pinches the back of my neck.

"You think ya brother sucks dick at surfing? Gotta check out my boy Sam here."

I smile, prying off his cold, wet grip.

"What we call you back then, Sam?"

"I gotta go, man. Don't remember."

"FlotSam! Yeah, that was it. FlotSam. Guy would paddle out at Topaz and just sit there, staring at the fuckin' pelicans for chrissake. Never did catch one wave did you, pal?"

The gleam in their eyes is something so pure. If I could bottle it, I'd be swimming through gold coins. I wouldn't call it hatred but...they need guys like me. Their life cycle is incomplete without a Sam.

I can't walk away fast enough. "See you guys tomorrow."

The two-beer limit is because I get my kid after school—all the time now, really. Sammy Junior. I wanted to name him after my favorite writer, but Heather wouldn't go for it. She said it had to be a name of someone important. She never could understand the beauty of words upon words, but we never talked about books. So, I gave the poor kid my father's name. Just like me. Just like a million other clucks on this spinning ball.

I inherited the beach house when Mom passed a few years ago. Place is more of a shack than a house. Built by my great-grandfather, mere steps away from monster power lines that terrorize the slopes of Anita Street. Yeah, you can see the ocean just over the King Harbor sign beyond the refinery. Prime real estate. Sometimes I'd go weeks without even staring at the view. Months. I bet some poor sap in Montana does the same thing with his big lousy sky.

Salt air has debilitated the deadbolt, but I pretend to unlock it for all my peeping neighbors. Sammy's room was my old room. After taking a shower, I usually nod off in his bed. The scent of his pillow reminds me when he was first born. *Happiness.* Heather was studying to be a nurse; I was loading boxes into UPS trucks. Worked overnights, mainly for the health benefits. That meant I had Sammy most days.

Somewhere along the line, things went bust. Sammy and I were fine, but Heather couldn't take it. Got into pills; dropped out of nursing school. Resented how Sammy would run to me whenever we shook the walls with our screams. What did she think would happen? I couldn't hold the boy without him clawing for a titty. I had to feed him that chalky formula. All those chemicals mixed up in her swelled bosom—bitch was a hundred percent poison, I swear.

She took a bartending gig at the Bac Door Lounge on Artesia after we split. Judge granted me full custody because I could "hold" a job, no criminal record. Read in the *Daily Breeze* that one of her friends got murdered a few months back. Sweet girl. Gone thanks to some drifter with a crooked hard-on. Haven't heard from Heather since then. I'm sure she's fine, drawing pints, hamming it up with the same burnouts every day. Be nice if she'd call the kid more often, but life scrapes the flesh off us all sometimes.

I try to think things would be different if we'd never met that summer on the Strand. Probably not though. Turned out just like my folks. Same house, same view—same mess. If not Heather, then some other poor gal walking out that front door carved by my great-grandpa.

But our kid would've been named Fante. That's for damn sure.

* * *

The street names crack me up. Always have. Emerald, Garnet, Ruby, Pearl. As if they could bedazzle a turd. I meet Sammy at the Redondo Library every day after school. I tell him that it's easier to do homework there, but the truth is that it's time for me to get lost. Maybe it was all that thinking about Heather earlier, but now I must visit my old pal, Bandini. They only have a few Fante novels, and I've creased them all to hell. Bandini had a shit situation too, only in Colorado. Made it out west and drowned like the rest of us. At least he had the balls to take a journey. How was he supposed to know about Los Angeles—its dreaded undertow, slowly sucking you in?

Sammy shows up twenty minutes late, but I don't fret. Kid's sharper than his old man. He's wearing these thick sunglasses I got him last Christmas. Never wears the suckers, so I know something's up. I don't ask when taking his backpack but can tell he's been crying (he's got Heather's eyes). We sidle up to our far spot in the corner, away from all the vagrants stinking up the joint. He tries to seep into his math book, but I tap the sunglasses. They slide down, revealing a plum for an eye. He doesn't want to talk about it and assures me everything's okay. I know how he must feel. My heart aches. I whisper a dirty joke about two lawyers walking on the beach, and he cracks a smile. The silence between us is fine because we're in a library. Bandini fills my brain, and Sammy hammers another equation. Today, we get lost together.

Tonight the fish are biting, but Denny spots a stray mako shark, so we pull anchor and motor around to the rear of Catalina. Moonlight silhouettes the island, turning its swirling tides into glitter. A team of buffalo is sprawled across one of the bluffs. Sharpening my blade, I nearly nick a finger when I see them. Poor bastards brought here for some dumb movie a hundred years ago, and now they're stuck. No stampedes. No killing cowboys and Indians. Just eat, fight, fuck and die—all in the same spot. But I'm sure the movie turned a profit. Someone should really airlift them home.

The six bank clerks on deck treat the buffalo like my shack's view, never once looking up from their tallboys. They're nice enough guys; twentysomethings that work at a Chase off Torrance Boulevard. Denny made friends with a few while opening a new savings after his second wife bailed. Thinks the dudes can print money, or something. Takes them to the Bull Pen once a month for well drinks and cougar hunting. Doesn't realize the kids probably want nothing to do with him—like everybody else.

Begged me to loan him two grand last year. I guess one of these financial wizards got wind of some new stock. I felt like God watching Denny's eyes glisten, unsure if I would help "save his life." Ended up giving him a thousand. Figured it might wedge some distance between us for a bit. Never asked if he'd invested it. Didn't care. If I had known then that we'd get fired from the Sport King, I never would've done it. Another poor decision to add to the list. I bet those movie execs would feel remorse too if they weren't all cold and dead, but alive on this boat, gazing out at their poor decisions clinging to a bluff. Then again, I guess the world needs dreamers.

Charlie's Place divides like a boys and girls co-rec dance once Denny invites his banking brothers for breakfast. It's not like the joint is some locals-only establishment like most places in town. Got two bucks? Here's a brew! At least that's what I like to think. The casuals get antsy whenever they see new blood this early in the a.m. Rusty's tab might not be the whale's bladder everyone has come to relish. Denny knows this, but also knows that no one will give him any shit to his face. He acts every part the big man, spotting the boys' rounds, securing the good table by a crustacean-filled piling.

I grab my two and hit my nook. First pull is extra salty; a couple of scales must've dropped out my beard. Used to gross me out when I first started, but now they're small beans. Funny how you learn to love stuff. I catch my reflection on the side of a dented napkin holder. Try to remember the last time I saw my face clean-shaven. Rusty is passed out on his bench, grimy hands balled on a pink belly, heavenly content. One of the guys puts glasses made of bendy straws on his face, a plastic cup for a hat. He snores us a soundtrack as we watch Denny be Denny. I let sunrays bake my whiskers.

Bandini. The scoundrel. I could never be that sharp. Ah, well. I do have some talents though. Got sponsored for skateboarding back in the day. E.T., a shop in Hermosa, believed that I might have the goods to go pro. I didn't...but at least someone thought so. Sure, I couldn't surf but I could skate like a madman. No one will tell you that. Kick-flip. Three-sixty flip. Big spin. You name it—I could do it. Off stairs. Rails...but that fire burned out.

Nowadays, my only gift you'd say is with faces. Only ones in the South Bay though. Pick a face—any face on the street. I can ballpark their future. Take this library for instance. Over there— little blondie with her unicorn Trapper Keeper? She'll end up at Texas Loosey's, serving prime rib in a bikini and leather chaps; a dimple on the ass for every lost college credit or abortion.

That freckled boy, screaming at Mommy's white flip-flops? He'll be okay. Lose a brother or best friend though—someone close. A preventable maritime accident. Go on to work the docks or construction, but only after years of couch surfing, living Rastafari-style.

There's really nothing to it. My gift to the world. Everyone bears the faces of their parents, right? Their parents' parents. Around here, that soft, beachy look always petrifies over time. Thousands upon thousands to be set in stone. Yeah, if there's one thing I'm sharp at...

Sammy, approaching with a king-sized dictionary, jars me back. He's supposed to be studying marsupials. Pages slide from my eyes to see what the deal is. That plum has turned into a leaky prune, magnified by his reading glasses. Patience isn't my virtue. I bite.

"What's up?"

Sammy doesn't skip a beat, finger-scrolling for something foreign. "Just curious 'bout something."

"Tell me the word. Fat chance I'll know."

"You wouldn't."

"Try me."

A gentle sigh escapes as he cracks. "Flotsam."

Like a cow prod to the gut. I swear. "Where'd you hear that?"

"Skyler—"

Denny's brat.

The words come and I can't stop them. "He call you that or what?"

Sammy's shoulders bounce, eyes locked on his finger.

He knows.

I could slap a nun—a whole gaggle of 'em. Right. This. Second.

I avoided Denny all night but the idiot doesn't even realize it. Wonder if the folks on board could feel the tension. Doubtful by their jovial grins as we dropped them portside earlier. Denny is gliding the boat out a gas station as I chop bait for the day crew. King Harbor is a speck in the distance; sun blips crown the entire coast. Beauty.

Gulls fight over entrails I toss overboard. Smells like low tide. Haven't been this upset in a long time. Maybe since I caught Heather on the lifeguard tower with that quarterback in high school.

No. I take that back.

Last year, this new guy came aboard the Sport King. Some kid from Palos Verdes; thought if he grew a beard long enough, none of us would see the silver spoon in his mouth. A slummer. It pissed me off, man. Here I am, struggling for years in this muck of mediocrity, trying to form the life I have: so-called friends—brothers. And here's this PeeVer, trying to infiltrate the common man, see how it is—try it on for laughs.

I showed him. All that grunt work, all day long—six back-breaking weeks. The fellas began to put him in his place at Charlie's too. It was great. One Monday he'd had enough, stood up to me. I popped him a good one, right in his gold-bricked nose. Didn't go down like I'd thought he would—hands without calluses always make me brazen. What did I know about fighting anyway? Been the nail my whole life, never once the hammer.

Denny tore the kid off me. Had to get eleven stitches and a CAT scan. That was the last time I felt this way. Not even that drawn-out custody mess, or Sammy having to tell a judge who he wanted to live with riled me this much.

Denny approaches with soft eyes, and says, "Yo, we gotta talk."

Here it comes. He should apologize for his kid and fill me in on what the beef is with Sammy. I'm sure he won't. Bet he doesn't have a clue. But the world needs dreamers same as this place needs guys like me. I toss guts to the wind.

As Denny prepares his speech, I notice the sunrise is now streaking purples and pinks—the clouds have eyelashes. Seals howl at us from atop a buoy. The scene nearly softens the rage.

Then Denny speaks. "Those guys—my boys from Chase—say that there's a big opportunity about to hit the market and…"

I tune out, a cauldron boiling behind my eyeballs. Can't even revel in Denny's nervous tic—licking chapped lips as if they were gum drops. I am no longer here—numb to this wrinkle-in-time replay. Denny notices that I'm not paying any attention. He reaches to tap my shoulder. I block his touch. It's only once I

135

see the blood that I realize which hand I had brought up and out...

...straight through Denny's hairy neck.

After all these years at being a sail bird, the fillet blade in my fist is purely an extension of my arm. Can practically gut with my eyes closed. Haven't sliced myself in years. I watch movies with creeps twirling machetes or tossing switchblades through beating hearts and think: *I could fucking do that.*

Slasher movies, however, don't need to spew all the blood.

The eyes are the most gruesome. I watch Denny's sparkle as he gurgles for my help. My gift to the world is gone at this moment, his face a rare anomaly that I can't forecast. We bled out a swordfish in this exact spot once, bludgeoned him first, though. I take destiny into my hand, reaching for that wooden club we keep around for such trying occasions. Denny's lifeforce whirlpools through every deck drain, mixing with fish and squid blood, one and the same.

Soon as I swing the club to his temple, it feels too good to stop. I've imagined this scenario since first grade, since that time he tripped me in front of Jenny Birch for no reason whatsoever. I indulge myself, exorcising decades of torment.

But every beast has his limit...

I drink in the horizon until I catch my breath and my heart rate softens. Closest possible witnesses are all gliding through kelp. Manning the hose, I scrub the deck before guiding the boat into port.

Back at Charlie's, I tell the crew that Denny said he had to split. They don't even question me, faces trapped inside plastic cups. Like I would've told them that his empty carcass slid gently into the Pacific—or better yet, that I was bailing town for good. I skip any food and just get my Bud Lights. The view from my nook feels off. Something's not right (other than the obvious). I take down half a cup and let some beer dribble onto my chest.

Most of the guys are just standing around, chain-smoking. *Rusty.*
My eyes dart to the bench. Hadn't even noticed the poor guy wasn't there. Knew something was off. The guys begin to bark about that time they brought a keg to the ninth hole of Sea Aire Golf Course. They laugh through glory, embellishing a rather mundane summer night.

All I see is the bench. That long empty bench. My mind wanders. I picture Rusty, dying in some white-walled hospital room, fluorescent bulbs acting as his heaven. I shake it off, think positively. He's on a motorcycle, some heavyset gal squeezing his ribs. They're tearing through Santa Barbara wine country, emerald hills aglow for miles. His beard splits from the sheer velocity as he hits the gas, revealing a gap-toothed grin on a road to somewhere. Rusty. You lucky devil.

I absorb the surroundings. My friends. Their faces. Time is now a factor that I cannot ignore.

The can of shaving cream in my bathroom is corroded, so I use a bar of soap. I wash my fillet blade and sharpen it. The knife knows what I'm thinking. Should've stopped and bought razors. With each scrape, the layers peel. Every one a painful slap into being. Takes about twenty minutes, and the end product is startling. I gaze into the mirror, fingers stroking hardened lines around my mouth, puffy cheeks—a new mole. Of all the faces...how could I have been so off about this one?

I load my father's old army sack with clothes for both of us. Sammy has a few favorite toys that barely fit. I think about Heather. Our life savings used to be rolled into this pickle jar atop our dresser. Mine is neatly splashed inside a metal tackle box in the garage. I split its contents in two, jamming wads into each front pocket. Should be enough for six months—maybe a year. Least until I can secure work. I wedge a book of matches into a crease in the front door, hoping it will stay shut. I'm sure the neighbors will try to notify me of any funny business, though. Nothing inside is of value anymore.

I wonder how the South Bay will be without a Sam. How long will it take for anyone to notice I've checked out? Who am I kidding? There will always be someone willing to fill my slot, take my nook—drink my two beers. Stepping down the front steps to the sidewalk, I pause to take in the view.

Sammy barely recognizes me. Doesn't know what to think when I tell him that homework doesn't need to be done today. He's still donning those sunglasses, and it hits me: He is nearly a man.

At the bus bench out front of the library, he grills me about the army duffel and everything it entails. I apologize for the surprise but tell him that we're hopping a plane out east. Colorado. We're starting a journey—our own journey. One where we'll know exactly how we got to wherever we end up. He asks about the house...Heather. I assure him they'll both still be here, but we have to go.

"What about school, Dad?"

"There's school all over, kid. Ain't just in classrooms."

He doesn't understand, but that's okay. I'm all out of dirty jokes. He'll get it somewhere along the way, maybe Portland or Seattle—age sixteen or thirty.

On the road, I'll tell him about everything: my life, meeting Heather, love and its madness, false brotherhood, Rusty and his endless emerald hills. I'll introduce him to Bandini and see if they get along. Worst case scenario? The boy goes it alone if they ever pile enough evidence to take me in. I am fine with that. As long as Sammy is out there—searching for an identity that isn't a birthright. The only gifts I can give him are infinite possibilities. Today his face doesn't look like mine anymore. It's uniquely Sammy.

The bus glides down PCH, onward to LAX. I turn to watch the asphalt flowing behind us, an old habit from too many boat wakes. That's when I see the seagulls and pelicans. Hundreds if not thousands, cast up in the sky like a giant tuna net. The spark of South Bay discord. They're heading our way amongst towering palms with fronds sharp as bait hooks. They know what's happening, trying to reel us back. I don't blame them either.

Everything is beautiful out west.

Rough Tender

Even at dusk, the heat baked through Beto's worn soles, toes writhing for comfort every few seconds under Fremont's blanket of lights, winking flirtations to unleashed tourists as he stood there speechless, hour ten, passing cards to drunkards not yet penniless, beyond primal, fiending for something more sordid than this. Obscene visuals couldn't free him from his mind. Bad thoughts. Girlies gyrated in dental floss, tossing beads to kiddos. Kentucky fried wives zip-lined across the sky; jumbo asses seeping through harnesses. All filler to aching eyes. A NASCAR couple sped past his outstretched arm, the woman pickled, scoffing, too righteous for the gesture; her man would take one late night, after she passed out. A teen approached and swiped, ultimately tossing the card to gawk at Glitter Gulch bosoms. Beto watched as it fluttered back to Earth, sliding into deep-fried Twinkie paste beside him. *Is that a sign?* Had she finally parted the veil only to reach for him through this object's grace at this very second? *No.* His Carmen despised this "horrible pandering." He grabbed another stack out the satchel and solicited sex.

The ads ran out after midnight. Didn't matter, downtown Las Vegas was oversaturated with passers now, most he knew, coworkers in bright *Babes to You!* T-shirts. He headed toward Binion's, looking for Ivan. Wanted to say *hey* before heading on. The street was a clusterfuck of superheroes and celebrities. Seemed like one day they all just appeared. Ivan said there was a crackdown in Hollywood, so they hopped Greyhounds or something. Tourists paid cash for prime pics of hilarity: Liza Minnelli hoisting a bachelorette dick wand, Wolverine clanking forties with bikers. Beto wondered if he could pull it off, anxious more than ever for fast income. *Would anyone want a picture with Fernando Valenzuela?*

Ivan waved under a monster steak and shrimp poster. Beto waded through cigar smoke to shake hands. Ivan was a survivor, like he and Carmen. He'd used a boogie board to glide up the coast to freedom. They traded barbs: Ivan mocking his long hair, Beto trashing faux jewelry. Smiles washed their faces for the first time today. Ivan asked about Carmen as he flicked cards at strangers. Good days and bad. They jabbed each other like crabs before Beto sped home.

Carmen.

Electric glitter faded to dark and he couldn't help but think of her, trekking past rows of bail bond shacks and boarded-up businesses. Stepping over a sleeping vagrant reminded him of their first nights in town, clasping each other under the stars, pretending to be vacationing campers for weeks. She'd do those silly faces to make him laugh, forgetting. Always the same, since they were children. Just like their dream; a healthy, loving family. All girls. That's what she would say, all the time, before. Thirty-one years was simply too short for fruition. God was calling to her. He moved quickly, praying in soft whispers.

Their dream home was Room 16 at the Velvet Elvis Motel. Despite a constant influx of questionable characters, never could they've imagined a home with a pool. This one was filthy and dry; local skateboarders frequented its guts but, *dios mio—* a pool! Beto headed for his door, looking away as a young girl got chewed out by some *flaco* in a cracked leather jacket. Sounded like they needed money too.

The jangling key usually woke her. An empty bed greeted; cigarette burns marred the carpet. He rushed to the bathroom. She lay motionless, head draped over the tub. He whisked her to the bed, dabbing blood from her lips with their towel. She hardly blinked, softly smiling before another spell. He squeezed, stroking her spine. She paused, towel at her lips. He kissed a hand. Bones.

She whimpered, "*Mi amor.*"

"DEREK!"

The blonde twirled a tiny straw from out her Lemon Drop, twitching as if she couldn't hear.

He leaned in, "Derek—nice to meet you."

She smiled, turning from his open palm.

He brushed it off. Deafening trance beats were killing his game. At least the Asian tugged his shirt before leaving. *Giggled an unhealthy amount though.* He choked back Disaronno, vowing no more booze with catchy commercials.

Once out the club, he sparked a Philly amongst chiming penny slots. Blue hairs swarmed on scooters. This was Vegas, how could he not find a nice girl down to party? They were everywhere, all types, living it up, laughing, cursing—succumbing to everything but his charm. Through the casino, he caught glimpses of fingers and snickers. *What the fuck?* These shredded jeans set him back three bills alone. *Haters.* He poked his aviators and puffed away, careful not to inhale, living large.

That ten in the mall got him though—his style. Drop dead, sold him these damn shoes. He posted at an outdoor beer booth. A pierced honey squirmed on a box under flashing bulbs. Was all good till he fixated on her scars. He leaned into the bar, slushing margaritas churned hypnotic. A Dos Equis slid before him, harboring concern. Bartender pointed to a troop of ladies at the far end. He tipped the bottle, lowering the shades to blast eyebrow lines. The short one approached.

"Hi there."

"Hey—thanks for the brew. I'm D—"

"Wait. Don't tell me. We got this funny thing going where

we're trying to spot celebrities out here—you a UFC guy or something?"

He chuckled, "Nah, that's just the shirt—you know? Mad style, right? What's your name?"

"Oh...no. That's all. Thanks."

He turned to see her crew busting in the distance. Shorty laughed so hard, could barely stay in her flip-flops. Bartender smiled, shaking his head. He shrugged, invincible till the dancer's scars began laughing too.

He headed toward the Nugget. Nearly one and the night was done. Just wanted to sleep it off, be fresh for that pool party at the Palms. Every ten feet, escort cards were flicked at him: Sin City butterflies. Richard Simmons cooed a pink boa as Cher chugged Four Loko beside him. He contemplated Glitter Gulch but kept on; already dropped a note there this morning. Had enough dimpled thighs and empty eyes. Playtime was over.

Shoes flung off once he breached the room, white pointy tips a bit scuffed. No chocolate on the pillow, welcomed by a long black strand. *Maid must've taken a snooze.* He reclined, flipping through futile channels before settling on *Cops*. Another bad habit he couldn't kick: with television came sleep.

Crackhead banter kept him awake. The clock claimed he'd only drifted for twenty. He went for a glass of water, kicking a shoe on the way over. A crusted card stuck to the bottom. Must've stepped in something sinister; smelled like Twinkie. He analyzed the card. *Babes to You!* Rate was reasonable—toll free number. A cheap blonde puckered wet lips, chest out, eyes loopy. Dug the rose on the back of her hand. He took a deep breath by the window, gazing down at the river of lights, imagining endless possibilities at the tip of his finger.

Margie didn't need to pull in the driveway to see it. The monster lock on the front door was visible from the street. *So, it had finally come to this.* Luckily, she'd moved everything to Mother's over the past weeks. Her bed was still inside, but she'd manage. Was worried about Lord Byron though, the Siamese she'd adopted, few months ago. Figured he'd run back here. All the others were fine at Mother's: Snickers, Bella, Jinx, Bojangles, Dame Priscilla. Closest she'd had to kids, so far. Pretending brought warmth to the heart. *Someday.*

In the rearview, a swarthy man approached, shotgun slunk at the shoulder. She put the minivan in park and craned her neck out the window. "Well, they finally did it, Bobby."

"Bastards came by this mornin'. Sorry, Margie."

"Aw hell, problems in all places."

"Damn shame."

Margie's headlights beamed bleakness. They drank in the empty block: busted windows, vacant driveways, yellow grass.

"Looks like a hurricane tore this fucker."

"Yup, just me now—last man standin'."

"How you holding up?"

"Good till 'bout three every mornin'—that's when they come. Stole copper out the light poles even. Fuckin' animals."

She shook her head. "Ain't seen Lord Byron out and about, have you?"

"Nope."

She grimaced, hoping them scavengers hadn't eaten the poor feline. "Well, you keep safe, Bobby. You see Byron, give me a call. Gotta get to work."

"So long, Margie."

The minivan rolled through moonlit shadows, back toward the charged row in the distance.

She parked at the building's rear, a weathered medical plaza now infested with perverse hot lines. Still couldn't believe that this was life now. From teaching kindergarten to call girl customer service; thanks for nothing, UNLV. *Only Temporary*: her mantra the past six months. She waddled through a maze of cubicles, all walks in headsets, barking orders at customers or escorts. She fastened her head piece under fluorescent tubes. Before taking a call, her twentysomething supervisor knocked at the grey partition.

"Talked to Roger 'bout that management gig. Liked the idea, sleeping on it for the time being."

"Oh...where is he? Haven't seen him in a while?"

"Holiday in Ibiza this time." His eyes rolled. "Anyway, said it's between you and Coco."

She adjusted her floral blouse. Coco? *Girl could barely buy alcohol.* "Thanks for that, Herb."

"Don't mention it—need a favor though, Margie."

"What's that?"

"Need you to pay this passer and let him go. Not a big deal—prolly be doing stuff like this if you get the promo—just business."

"What he do?"

"Nothing. Big shots are forcing Roger to increase turnover for passers—cut 'em after two months now. So many coming out here for work, you know? They say it keeps the overhead under control—streamlines the business model. Guy's in the waiting room. Make sure he leaves his shirt behind, okay? Roger had to put a freeze on those too." He handed an envelope containing three crisp fifty-dollar bills.

She turned toward the waiting room. The sight sank her gut: Beto on a chair, hands devouring his face. He'd been hired the same day she was. They'd become good friends. She took a deep breath and contemplated how to break it. *Problems in all places?* Herb returned with one last request.

"Before you do that, grab the info from the guy on line six—then call Julia and send her over."

"She's got the night off though."

"Not after Roger caved on the new cards—haven't seen 'em yet?" He tossed one from his pocket onto her desk.

Babes to You! Julia puckered back at her. "Oh, okay. Not a problem."

He winked. "You're a doll, Margie. Thanks."

She leered back at Beto, expelling a deep sigh.

Julia reclined on the stained couch, arms out, fingers splayed, wondering whether the new black-tipped nails made her look like a model or a mechanic. The rose on her right hand bled from age, needed a touch up. She grabbed her favorite bong (Iggy) and began packing a bowl. A toke was interrupted by Oakenfold beats, chiming louder and louder. She searched for her cell amongst a table of McWrappers. Nearly crushed one of the Yorkies as she swatted lingerie piles on the carpet. The beat peaked, then nothing.

"Da fuck you at, fucka."

One of the dogs began to yap.

"Shut up, Whiz!"

The beat started back up.

"Sheeit." She made for the bathroom, beside the heaping ash tray. "Hello?" The voice on the other end shut her eyelids. She went back to Iggy.

"But I got da day off, Margie. Roger don't know what da fuck dat means? No fuckin' *trabajo* fo' dis ho!"

Margie's high pitch had her hold the phone at a distance, reanalyzing those tips before hearing enough. "Listen, I don't care where he at—*you* know why I need da night off, Margie. Bjorn's flyin' in dis mornin'—gotta have everythin' just right, awright? You dunno how hard it is to get a good man, Margie. No offense, but I bet da dudes you be fuckin' wit is straight *dawgs*."

Margie stammered.

"Dis be da new fucker eHarmony be doin' me wit, Margie. Flyin' in from *Sweden*, Margie! SWEDEN! Dis pussy so good, fools be burnin' passports, okay? So, you tell mothafuckin' Rog dat any other night I'm game, but tonight—nah, ain't hatnin'." She tried ending the call without smudging a nail but magic words brought it back. "Wait—what? *New cards*...You serious

now—don't be playin'?" She squealed. "Oh, my God. Fuckin'
Rog—what a man, dat mothafucka. Awright, awright—send a
car over in thirty...Wait—what? Dude's named *Derek*? How
you spell dat?"

She stood there, bleached lock in the corner of her grin.
Babes to You! She was *the* babe. Her body slithered its way to
the bedroom. Roger deserved a proper fuck. Teasing that puss
paid off, sometimes. She flicked the light switch; two children
and a toddler, snoozing on a twin.

She clapped. "Get da fuck up, y'all. Time a go see Grampa!"

The oldest, about eight, swiped crust from her eyes.

Julia fretted over an outfit. Wanted to wear those new stilettos
but her big toe jutted out, sharp, dirt jammed beneath. Didn't
have enough for a pedi.

The oldest appeared in the doorway.

"What you doin'? Gotta hurry, get dem dressed."

"Hungry, Momma."

"It be breakfast soon, okay. Grampa got stuff fo' ya."

"Na-uh. Last time he made us pickle sandwiches."

"Those was my favorite, girl. Don't be picky." She swapped
lace underwear. "Git a move on!"

The girl slunk in defeat, heading back to the bedroom.

Julia giggled, loading a purse with flavored condoms, curious
which picture Roger put on those cards. Didn't matter. They
were all damn sexy.

The entire office took notice. Margie closed the door, shutting
blinds. Beto sat bare-chested, sobbing into the faded T-shirt. If
only she'd known before relaying the news. *Poor Carmen.* Such
a lovely woman: a veterinarian's assistant back in Mexico.
Margie would bring over Jinx and Bojangles whenever they'd
stop eating: a mountain of maternal stress. Short, simple words
would soothe all worries, saving the bank account and the
mind. She'd invited them to her home on several occasions.

Dinner as gratitude. Remembered how both would marvel at her plush furniture, gasping at the Olympic-sized pool and its blueberry lights. *Gosh, I miss it all.* They even praised her white girl enchiladas. *Why didn't I just serve steaks?* Carmen mentioned illness as if it were a blister. Never had she known. This sudden decline was unreal. Her brain clicked back to present, mantra taking hold. *Only Temporary—Only Tempo*...She peered through slats at Herb, yukking it up with Coco-the-ditz, patting her hairdo, praising its body. There was only one option.

They bolted through the parking lot. Beto's tears dried from confusion. Margie fumbled car keys as Herb shouted threats from afar, a T-shirt pom-pom overhead. She ignored everything, turning to Beto once the doors were unlocked. "Get in."

She gunned through downtown backstreets, careful not to clip inebriated nomads. The Velvet Elvis beaconed busted neon. Beto led the way. Lost souls cluttered the flight up. Margie stared at the decrepit pool; another dagger to the heart. The door flung open. She went in first.

The day Margie's father passed, she'd just turned thirteen. Her senses took a snapshot of the environment. Could still see his dry tongue clamped on tubes. The scent: stale lemon sanitizer, a hint of bile. Death seemed so bright under maximum wattage. This motel room was the antithesis. One look at Carmen and she knew the score.

"We have to get her to a hospital," came under her breath.

Beto didn't break his bedside prayer.

Margie sat beside her, stroking wet hairs on her brow. Carmen looked porcelain in slumber, angelic. *Would a hospital even take her? If so, do they deport the sick?* Her mind raced, exhausting options. *Who could possibly help, even in the slightest?*

The knock came as fresh rays spoked the casino skyline. Derek used the peephole to peruse his purchase. *Same as the card, just as ordered.* He opened up.

After a brief introduction, Julia tossed her purse on the bed and kicked off shoes. Derek gazed at her grimy feet, heels crusted with months of dead cells. Rose on her hand was a jumbled blot. *We've all been teenagers.* Pulling out a pipe, she regaled rates while packing a bowl. He took it all in, the visual, pausing toward the door before accepting the company.

"You know, I really just want to watch you dance."

A blue plume expelled, sparking wet coughs. "Honey, I *don't* dance."

"Okay, um, how 'bout we just...talk—I'll pay you. No need to leave just yet."

Her eyebrow peaked, ultimately going lax with a *fuck it* implication. She torched a menthol slim. "Sure, baby. Whateva gets you off. If dat be da case, I gotsta use the commode."

Derek wiped his face, wondering why the fuck he ever invited such a mess. Obvious *plops* and *splats* had him rushing to crack a window. The glass slid barely two inches. Suicide prevention here was for rock bottom gamblers. He smirked, acknowledging peculiar cases, such as this.

A hearty flush and running water brought on some comfort. Julia sat back down, smacking her lips, wiggling toenails. "Where yoos from?"

"Reno. Here on business."

She gave an up-down. "You a fighta or somethin'?"

"Nah—got my own metal shop. Ain't *that* glamorous."

"Huh."

"What about you?"

"I dunno—giving out personal info just don't sit right—in dis sitchiation, ya dig?"

His hands shot up. "That's fair. I mean, just trying to make conversation. Don't wanna get too personal." He smiled. *And here, ramming his dick into her ass could be fully accommodated.* He switched gears. "What do you think of my clothes— honestly? You get a lot of clients dressed like this?"

Her lips pursed. "Ugh...nah—you be da first. Why you axe?"

"Been gettin' dissed by every girl in Vegas. Wonderin' what the fuck's wrong."

"Well, fo' starters—looks like you be tryin' too hard. How old a you?"

"Thirty-nine."

"Dat shirt's made fo' pimple poppers. You a grown ass man, okay? What's with da facial hair and brow lines?" She cackled. "Still listenin' to Hammer?"

"Don't hold back now." He smirked. "Least you're honest. I...I just thought it went with the package, you know?"

"Listen, fix dat shit. Da face ain't dat bad, don't be 'fraid to show it. Gotta be yo' 'self, dat's all. Bitches love an honest man—confident. Not some foo' in a getup screamin' phony. Grab some nice button-ups—slacks—who knows, might not be payin' fo' top shelf puss no mo'."

They paused for a beat. Her gold tooth glistened as she offered the pipe. He humored. Within minutes, they were giggling through exotic topics.

Room service wheeled in eggs, coffee and a mountain of bacon. Their dynamic didn't faze the busser. Had seen it all out here. They carried on in mouthfuls.

"Got a family?"

He slurped the mug, head shaking. "Tryin'."

"I gots a few kids."

"Must be great, huh? I mean, you're a better person because of it—right?"

"Shit, honey—you tell me. I gets paid to suck an' fuck. Ain't no mom a da year award fo' dis ho."

"Where's Dad?"

"They three baby daddies. One's a jailbird, ain't gonna see his ass fo' sho'. Other two done up an' gone. Ain't no thang."

"Clients?"

"Da fuck?"

"Were they your clients?"

"Fuck nah." Her emotion subsided, realizing merit to his

question. "Got a new boo doh—*Swedish.*"

"How'd you meet."

"Interweb—you know, computa? Sheeit, supposed to be grabbin' his ass from da airport right now."

"Why aren't you?"

"You pay for da night—I'm witchoo."

"I know but..."

"Ain't too big a deal. He call when his plane lands—I'll 'splain everythan'. See, dude who runs da service, Rog, put me on da new flyer—made me da babe of *Babes to You!* Figure, do him a solid. Come in on my day off."

Derek got up and retrieved the card atop the dresser. He held it up, comparing.

She grabbed it. "Oh snap, ain't seen dis yet."

He watched as she stared like a child hoisting a cereal prize. Small pools made her eyes diamonds. The smile slowly faded. She tossed the card at him and got back to breakfast.

"What's the matter?"

"Always thought it'd feel betta."

"What'ya mean?"

"You know, bein' somebody. Fame or whateva. I see dat and...I just dunno. Don't seem all dat big a deal."

"Big enough for me—else I wouldn't have called, right?"

She grinned through chipmunk cheeks.

Oakenfold beats blared out her purse.

"Your phone?"

"Oh, shit—*Bjorn.* Da new boo done arrived!" She dropped the fork and rummaged, grimacing at the cell before answering, "What's it now, Margie?"

The following minute became frantic. Derek watched as Julia paced, listening, body swelling to a state of alarm. When the call ended, he didn't have to ask. She laid it out, why their date was now over. Cannabis bliss seeped into the walls.

"Is there anything I could do to help?"

"I wouldn't axe fo' a ride if it wasn't a 'mergency. Gotta driva waitin' fa me in da casino, but if I show up befo' our time's through, he gonna call the bossman an' shit'll be fucked."

"Okay—don't worry. Not a problem. My work truck's in the garage. Got all your stuff?"

"Mm hmm." She swiped the last stick of bacon for the road.

Beto leaned down, planting a tender kiss. Carmen was awake, the pain had her quiet. Margie rose and tapped Beto the moment she saw Julia leap out the truck. Figured the driver was a friend. Urgency swamped minor details.

Julia barged in, pipe out, packed with a monster bowl. Last time Carmen was suffering like this, ganja worked wonders.

Beto propped Carmen for the medicine.

Derek tranced, refraining from questions. A lilac scent wafted beside him.

Their eyes met.

"Hi, I'm Derek."

"Margie." *Hand could use some lotion.* Then it hit. She hinged her jaw from going slack. *Derek—that Derek? Was too handsome for a john.*

Shoulders touched as they stood, quiet, watching a slight grin come over Carmen; her aura changed from grey to yellow.

Beto fingered the cross, eyes to the ceiling.

Julia and Margie approached Carmen's open palm.

"Betta, baby?"

Her fingers pinched the air.

"Dat's good."

Margie sat bedside, nostrils flaring.

Carmen smiled, *"Gracias."*

Beto gave Margie a hug, then Julia.

"Anythang fo' my friends, you know dat." She grabbed Margie by the arm. "I gotsta talk witchoo—outside."

Derek leaned on the balcony. Arid peaks stood sharp in the distance. He spied on Margie, moment she walked past. Got that strange twist in the gut. Been some time but still rang bells. He grinned, turning back to the peaks. *Could get used to this beauty.*

Julia took Margie to the stairs. "What's goin' down withcoo?"

"Roger had me fire Beto today."

"What—didju?"

"Well, yes and no. I quit right after."

"Sheeit! Mothufuckin' Rog—imma get buck wild on dat bitch—"

"That can wait, okay? Carmen needs to get to a hospital—should have seen her this time when I got here."

"You right—you right. Po' *baby.* But how—none us can help Beto afford dat?"

Derek approached. "I don't mean to eavesdrop, but I might be able to help."

"Whatchu gonna do?"

Margie shushed with a hand. "Let him speak."

"Julia knows I'm in town for business—see, I'm opening another shop here this week—in Henderson. Things are booming right now for us, and I could use a few more men. Beto could work for me, no problem—we offer full benefits. Is he legal?"

"Nah."

"Huh, might be able to work around that. Had a few guys start out the same way."

"What he be doin'?"

"Collecting scrap metal—manual labor mostly."

A hand shot to Margie's hip. "You ain't one of those guys who pays assholes to steal copper out of light poles, right?"

"Just the opposite—won a bid through the city to start fixing them, block by block. That's why we're expanding here."

"*Oh,*" she relaxed, "Don't suppose you need a secretary too?"

He smirked, "As a matter of fact...Julia—know anyone smart and gorgeous?"

Margie blushed.

Julia pecked Derek's cheek before heading back inside. "Don't trip, Margie." She pointed to her ass. "He ain't even have dis piece—jus' talked, all night long. Wouldn't shut da fuck up." She cackled. "Tella how you goin' ta buy new clothes, Derek." He laughed, deflecting. "So, how can I reach you—for the job."

"*Yeah*, the job."

They basked in an awkward glow, exchanging info, bodies tingling from the birth of new possibilities.

Julia watched on the balcony as Beto sobbed from Derek's good news, down by the truck. If only *her* life could work itself out. She quadruple-checked the cell for Bjorn's missed call. Plane had landed three hours ago. He promised to call. Never once had they spoken on the phone. *Maybe dat boy be shy?* She shook out the foolish thought, going back into the room.

Margie sat with Carmen, a bit more animated.

"But why no?"

"You act like I'm not trying, Carmen. The right one hasn't come along, that's all."

"*Mira mija*, I know—I know. But the big house a yorse needs kids—lotta them."

Margie couldn't tell her the home was gone.

"Me an' Beto, kids was everyting to us. We pray an' pray— but...no." Her hands shot out, "No now. But—*you now*." She grabbed Margie's palm, mumbling for Guadalupe.

Julia became a lightning rod. Here she was, fretting fake romance when true love already existed for her, times three. How could she have ignored her kids this long? She reloaded the pipe, placed it on the table and approached the women, arms out.

"*Mija*, where ju going?"

"Gotta pick up my babies."

Carmen smiled. "How old?"

Her hand shot belly high. "Youngstas—all girls."

Carmen clapped. "Pictures?"

"Not on me. Bring some ova tomorrow—be back wit mo' meds."

"Okay. Give them many kisses."

"You know I will, honey. Margie—call me, okay?" She turned toward the door and paused. "Hey, dat man down dere's a keepa, Margie. Ain't no straight dawg—balee dat!"

Margie approached the balcony, watching as Derek waved, taking Julia back to her driver. Those *Only Temporary* days were over. Needed a new mantra. *How 'bout...Act Two?* Sunshine touched her cheeks as Beto leaped onto the bed, telling Carmen of all the new blessings bestowed.

Tip the Barkeep

A lousy Tuesday night crowd became the least of Jimbo's worries the moment he hung up the phone. Two minutes ago, the day's worst seemed to be the Lakers only winning by ten, and Varla harping for complimentary Jäger at the far stool. All that was a foot massage now. Ricky was on the run. Sounded bad. Jimbo wasn't exactly sure what had happened, but he knew the kid was headed for the bar. "Just for a few hours, Jimbo," so he obliged. He was a softy for tight spots. If only hiding out fugitives brought about hefty tips.

Pat's II Cocktails held a corner spot off Pacific Coast Highway in the Avenues of Redondo Beach. It was a twenty-hour tavern, six to two, seven days a week, catering to veteran drunkards in the a.m. and freshman sippers by night. Locals dubbed it The Deuce. Jimbo's barkeeping skills around town eventually landed him here. It was an easy enough bar to run, strictly well hooch and bottles of beer. Without taps on draft, washing pints wasn't an option, just tumblers or high balls mostly. No heavy lifting. Jimbo never really shut the doors either. Still between places since his divorce, the cot in the supply room always kept him around. He let buddies swing by between closing and opening if they could check their rowdiness at the door. Such was the case tonight.

Varla strolled in around closing and grabbed her usual stool while Jimbo counted the register, shaking his head. He could remember when the twentysomethings could put a few back in this town. Seemed like every few years the new wave of kiddos got softer and softer. Shit, soon he'd be slinging straight cola. Varla hiccupped and giggled. She was a sight to say the least, and not in a dick chubbing way either. They had gone to Redondo High together back in the nineties. She was voted most popular—huge tits, butter face. Nowadays, her popularity came at a small price and was distributed in the men's stall or out back by the dumpster. Jimbo let her hang since nowhere else would. She was good people, surfing the waves of a crummy life, one shot at a time. He let her in on the Ricky situation, figuring she might have already heard. Word traveled fast in the South Bay, secrets the speed of bullets.

"Get outta here, man. You serious? I just talked to Sophie on my way over. She didn't say nothing."

"Prolly just happened, he sounded pretty scared." He popped himself a Sierra Nevada. "So, Sophie still keeps tabs on Ricky even though they broke up senior year, huh?"

"Guess they still fuck on occasion." She downed a shot.

"Do me a favor. Keep an ear out for the back door, not sure when he's gonna be here."

She smiled, pointing to the empty shot glass. He floated a goofy grin and filled it to the brim.

A good forty minutes passed before there was a rap at the back door. Jimbo heard it, running as fast as his giant gut would allow down the narrow corridor to the parking lot. The door clanked open but it wasn't Ricky. An elderly gentleman in a worn blue suit slapped him on the shoulder, sauntering in. "Hey there, Jimbo. How goes it?"

"Oh, you know, Doc. Shit could be better."

Varla perked up from the stool. The moment she saw who it was, she rushed over for a hug. "Hi, Doc—looking sharp, honey."

Doc Reeves was somewhat of a local celebrity. He was a certified physician, once prominent about town with community cable commercials and a softball tournament for the bar leagues. Nowadays, his two sons had taken over the practice, leaving plenty of time on his hands to socialize and dawdle while drinking. Jimbo let him pay off tabs with prescription pills. It supplied an overhead that made up for shit tips, like tonight. He had a neighborhood kid he supplied that sold to the evening sippers most nights. It was a small-time racket, but it kept him afloat.

The old man perched on a stool, removing four vials of pills from his coat and placing them on the counter. Jimbo searched each of their labels—three full of Vics and, ooh, one large Oxy. He might finally be able to put a down payment on that sailboat in the harbor. He poured Doc a tall Jameson and made for the phone. Doc and Varla canoodled. The kid picked up after one ring.

"Red, it's Jimbo. Got some supply for pickup. How fast can you get down here?"

"Gimme like thirty, man. Got a drop-off near Alta Vista."

"Cool, brotha."

Click.

Jimbo figured Varla, Doc and Red wouldn't fuck with the Ricky situation. They were harmless. Would mind their own. No big deal. Ricky probably wouldn't show for a while anyway, since he wasn't there by now. Caution was key, but money was king.

Varla and Doc were in a heated game of tabletop shuffleboard when the phone rang just after three a.m. Jimbo lowered the jukebox, putting the Descendents to a halt. He answered. Red was out back. He let him in, immediately asking if he'd heard anything about Ricky. Red dismissed the name with a shoulder shrug before saying, "Hey," to Doc and Varla. Guess word still wasn't out.

Jimbo slang the kid a High Life, a rarity at The Deuce

considering the boat derelicts wouldn't touch the stuff. Red stuck the bottle through his fireball goatee, draining half in two gulps. "So, where's the shit, man?"

Jimbo slunk under the counter, pulling the vials from beneath a pile of dishrags. Placing them on the counter, the kid's eyes grew large. He hoisted up the Oxycontin. "This oughta sell pretty fast."

"Hell yeah. Already know who's gonna want that whole thing."

"Right on. Same as always, alright? Seventy-thirty split, free drinks at the bar."

Red's face squished with distaste before chugging the rest of the bottle. "Yeah, okay. Can you get any more of the Oxies though? The clucks around here are fiending for 'em."

Jimbo turned to Doc, anxious at the end of the shuffleboard as one of his weights clanked through Varla's defense and dangled off the edge. "Doc, come here a sec."

"Yeah?"

"Can you get any more of these down here?"

Doc scratched his forest of gin blossoms. His sons had had his license revoked at the first of the year. He had forged a few of their prescription tablets to get these. "When you need them by?"

Red said, "Soon as possible."

"Lemme call Nathan—might have some back in the office. He could probably bring them down—gets into work about six."

Jimbo knew Nathan, broke the kid's nose in third grade. A solid prick forever, with the Ricky situation brewing, the last thing he wanted was that fuck in the place. Not like he would actually show though. He'd had enough of good ole Dad. "Nah, that ain't gonna work, Doc. I don't want any more folks coming down, if I can help it. Think you can run out and see what you can do?"

"Sure...sure. Lemme just have another quencher, for the road. Still got a key to the office, should work."

Jimbo tilted another long whiskey pour and thought about

his soon-to-be boat. What would he name it? Had to paint the bottom first, of course. Just before the top off, a barrage of loud knocks came from the back door. Red reached over for another brew when Jimbo left to answer.

This time it was *him*, the pale moonlight casting a glow across his slim face, giving it a ghostly definition. Ricky was clutching his left bicep, leaning against the doorjamb. Jimbo helped him in, guiding him to the rear stockroom before locking back up. Ricky sat on the cot amongst booze boxes piled high and a mini-TV. He was gently seeping tears of adrenaline. Jimbo told the others everything was okay before heading back to see what was doing.

"I fucked him up, man. Fucked him up *bad*."

"Who, Ricky? What happened?"

"Was partying down in Hermosa—Fat Face Fenner's—ran into Sophie's ex-husband."

"Carl?"

"Nah, Mick—the one used to smack her around. I dunno, guess I musta had a few too many, started mouthing off about Sophie. You know, dumb shit."

"So what happened?"

"Well, I was on my way home, walking down the Strand, checking out the waves, when the fucker popped outta nowhere— slashed at me with a blade." He removed his hand from his bicep, letting Jimbo see the gash. "I had to do it, man. It was self-defense."

Jimbo dabbed a clean rag on the opening, then squeezed to try and stop the bleeding. He didn't want to ask but had to. "What did you *do*, exactly?"

"You know, we got to tussling and, I dunno, eventually I got hold of the knife and hit him in the gut. Once wasn't enough though, Jimbo. I just kept cutting, man." His eyes began to re-well. "I just couldn't stop stabbing."

The taste in Jimbo's mouth was worse than any three-pack-a-day habit. Carving a man once in self-defense was one thing.

Ricky pulled out a smoke and lit up. "I think Chum-Bum saw me, man."

Jimbo knew the chubby old vagrant—hung out under the pier. "Are you sure?"

"Pretty positive, saw him running toward Hennessey's, hollering for help. Mick was bleeding pretty heavy on the sand. He knows me, man. My pops played ball with him back in the day—before he went batshit."

Jimbo tried to squash the panic, knowing that it would only cloud their thought process of what to do next. "I wouldn't worry about it. He's not exactly the most credible witness." At least he hoped not. "So, what's the plan?"

"I called Sophie. She knows. Said she'd pick me up at five and drop me off in Pedro. Hopper is working the day boat to Catalina on a Calico bass run, said he had room for me. Gonna hole up on the island for now. See what happens."

Jimbo's wheels kept turning. "Okay, that sounds like a plan. Let me grab one of the sweatshirts we have for sale so you can change out of that bloody shirt." He tied off the rag around Ricky's arm, met by a grunt. "When you head out there, Varla knows something is up. Just tell her it's nothing, okay?"

Ricky nodded and cashed the smoke on the ground. They heard the rear door open and close. Jimbo shook his head, letting Ricky know it was nothing. People could only get out, not in.

"Alright, I'll be right back."

Jimbo noticed that Doc had gone before he rummaged through the cabinets, looking for a large sweatshirt. He couldn't remember actually selling one of them over the years, wondering why he had ordered them in the first place. Red and Varla were now at the Golden Tee in the front corner, taking turns playing a simulated back nine. Varla smacked the holstered white ball, crashing her fingers at the screen, trying to curve a chip up and over a sand trap.

"Doc left, huh?'

"Yeah," said Red.

Varla cursed as her ball plunked into a pond. "That Ricky back there?"

Jimbo nodded, "He's fine," heading back to the stockroom with a first aid kit and the hoodie.

Ten minutes later, Ricky and Jimbo emerged from the stockroom with a pair of healthy grins. Varla gave Ricky a hug while Red paid no mind. Varla inquired about the situation. Ricky deflected.

"Ah, just some drunken bullshit. Thought I was about to get rolled for a drunk and disorderly."

She rubbed the nape of his neck, thankful it was nothing too serious.

Red made his way over, grunting at Ricky. The four of them commenced slouching around, retelling tall tales of their glory years, back when the city was golden and their dreams were relevant. Jimbo kept time. Five o'clock couldn't get there fast enough.

The walk to Reeves Medical from The Deuce was a brisk three blocks. It was in a second-story suite above a surf shop in the Hollywood Riviera; a cluster of blocks once frequented by yesteryear celebrities for beach activity, but no longer. Doc fiddled with his keys, adamant that one of them would unlock the front door. After trying all twelve, still no luck. Those bastard sons screwed him again, must have stolen the key or changed the locks. On his way back, he remembered an old friend he had bestowed an emergency key a few years back. She owned a twenty-four-hour diner across the way—Nancy's. He rushed across PCH.

Nancy was a short-haired woman of girth who never smiled a day in her life. He caught her out front tossing a pair of "loiterers" into the night for only ordering cups of coffee. These "delinquents" weren't even out of their teens yet, both brown, reeking of "the pot" and "bad for business." She stood out front of the tiny diner, hands on the hips in all her glory when she noticed him. "Doctor Reeves. Hungry?"

He peered inside the place, cluttered with tables and chairs. One customer sulked at the counter, poking a beyond questionable egg dish—The Wagon Wheel. He knew the man, a cop, frequented The Deuce on Fridays. A Negro cook scraped at the flatiron grill in the rear. Nancy reiterated the question, insisting he order something.

"Oh, no thank you, Nancy. I was just wondering if you still had that emergency key for the office."

She scoffed. "Nah, one of your sons picked it up a few months back."

"Rats," he mumbled. That went that.

"Anything else I can get ya—Wagon Wheel?"

He smiled, leering down at the customer, wondering what was wrong. He knew the man. They'd toasted drinks on several occasions. A good man, but a cop. "Maybe just a cup of coffee for now."

Nancy rolled her eyes and fetched the pot. Doc went toward the counter. The place smelled like a sour mop. He couldn't help but notice that the customer's inebriation had turned him into a buoy, bobbing atop his chair.

"Mike, right?"

The customer turned his bloodshot eyes, "Yeah?"

He stuck out his hand. "Doc Reeves."

The man quickly remembered, reaching for the grip. "Oh yeah, have a seat."

Nancy plopped a mug in front of him, splashing droplets on the countertop. She got back to shaving mold off slices of cake in the display case.

"Couldn't help but notice you looked a little down."

Mike tossed over the front page of the *Daily Breeze* atop a stool next to him. Doc scanned the paper and saw it. Mike pushed the greasy plate to the side. "Suspended without pay, indefinitely." He pulled a flask from out his coat and offered Doc a pull. Doc could see a revolver harnessed up under his armpit.

"Off the clock but still carrying, I see."

"Yeah." He pulled the .38 halfway out the holster. "They revoked my service pistol. This one's mine. Just feel naked without one, you know?"

Doc took a slug and continued reading the article. Looked like good guy Mike, a detective actually, got caught bludgeoning a witness while boozing on shift. Another black eye for the force. Still, nothing shocking. Doc watched as Mike drained the last of the rum, his eyes rolling back into his head.

"Let's say we get outta here, Detective."

"Where to?"

"Grab us a night cap and some breakfast beers—my treat." He tossed a twenty onto the counter. Nancy cursed under her breath. They left their orders to fend for themselves.

It was just after four thirty. Ricky was feeling no pain thanks to the three Vicodin he'd scored off Red. As a matter of fact, all of them had a couple downers now coursing their veins. Jimbo whipped up another round of shot concoctions he'd crafted in the wee hours over the years. He whizzed the martini shaker over four bucket glasses, back and forth, until every last drop found its fill.

"Now, this one I don't have a name for but it looks like diarrhea."

Varla laughed, "How 'bout The Squirts?"

"Sounds good to me," said Red.

They each cheered a glass, tossed them back, and were met with puckered faces.

The back door boomed, sending Jimbo off toward it. The moment he saw Doc's companion, he nearly got the squirts for real. "Hi, Mike. How you been?"

"Been better, my friend. Got too many nights off nowadays."

"I was about to say, you usually swing by Friday mornings."

Doc smiled. "Well, it's Wednesday now and damn near sunrise, my boy. We got some livers to pickle."

They stormed in, laughing.

Jimbo realized he was the only one, besides Doc, who knew Mike was a cop. Better to keep things calm and not mention it. The pills had Ricky a little less antsy now and he'd be gone in less than a half hour. He jumped back behind the bar as Doc introduced Mike to the gang. "The usual, Mike?"

"Yes sir, that'd be perfect."

He reached for the Bacardi 151.

Doc finished with, "And this here's Ricky."

"Nice to meet you—Mike."

Both men grabbed a stool. Doc leaned over the bar and blurted, "Couldn't grab those pain pills for you, Jimbo."

Jimbo widened his eyes, giving him a *shut-the-fuck-up* look. Doc suddenly realized his heightened stupor had let one slip.

Mike asked, "What you need pain pills for, Jimbo?"

"Oh, you know…" He scrambled. "My ma—got a bad back and stuff."

"Sorry to hear." He took a pull of rum. "You know what these kids are doing nowadays with those pain pills?" He paused, turning to his new friends, not knowing exactly how old they were. "Not you guys, of course—kids in the general sense. Anyways, we had a case few months back, young girl, Terry Swisher. Good gal, father owns the Laundromat off Knob Hill. Guess she had an addiction to those things…Oxy-something-or-others. Was crushing 'em up, snortin' and shootin' it like a rock 'n' roller. Damn shame, really. Parents found her slunk on the toilet. We had to come in and clean up the mess." He looked Jimbo dead in the eyes. "Never could understand it. Talk about throwing your life down the shitter."

Jimbo nodded in condolence, pouting his bottom lip. Doc

changed the subject.

"How 'bout that storm headed in?"

Jimbo casually wiped down the countertop until he was in front of Red. He scribbled on a napkin once Mike turned his back and slid it over.

Red's eyes were heavy, stomach growling from the shots. He read the note.

Mike's a cop
BAIL!

That woke him up. He rose from the stool, vials clanking in his pockets. "I think I'm out, Jimbo. Thanks for the beers, man."

"Don't mention it, partner. Just part of the deal. See you in here later tonight, right?"

"Sure thing, boss." He yelled, "Later everybody," before hitting the back corridor.

Varla convinced Ricky into a game of shuffleboard after reloading the jukebox. Mike was explaining to Doc the misfortunes that led up to his dismissal, when Jimbo chimed in. Mike filled him in after handing over the folded front page from out his suede jacket.

"Jesus, Mike. I'm sorry. Drinks on the house."

"Thanks. Hey, you got a TV around here? Kinda wanted to see if I made the early bird news."

"Yeah, let me grab it." He headed for the stockroom.

Jimbo placed the nine-inch tube on the bar in front of them. The ancient thing hummed into picture with a porcelain-faced Asian reporter. The three of them watched and drank through ten minutes of uneventful correspondence. An inner-city book club was news. After the break, there it was—Mike's mug hovering over the reporter's shoulder as she crucified him to the public with all the brutal details. Jimbo filled Mike's tumbler.

Behind them, Varla said, "Geez, Ricky. You're bleeding."

Mike and Doc turned around.

Ricky glanced down at the sweater, blood seeping slow. "It's nothing. Got scagged surfing yesterday."

Jimbo grabbed another sweater and pointed for him to meet back in the stockroom. Doc went to take a leak. Mike remained in front of the tube while Varla puffed out her chest, vying for attention. The TV spouted *Breaking News.*

"Would you look at that," Mike said. "Someone got murdered in Hermosa Beach." He couldn't help but think that he might have been on that case.

"What?"

Varla scooched toward him, way buzzed but curious. The reporter notified that a suspect was on the loose, possibly wounded as there was a blood trail leading from the crime scene. They watched as the Channel 4 newscopter reeled shots of search dogs following a scented trail on the beach. The victim was identified as Mick Gorso. Details of his demise were still under wraps. Varla's hand shot to her mouth. *Sophie's ex!* Poor thing. She was almost overwhelmed with sadness when it hit. Her brain clicked two plus two. Ricky hated that fucker. He had called Jimbo in a panic before she got there. Then the bleeding arm. *Oh no, please no. Ricky?*

Mike saw the horror on her face. "You know that guy or something?"

She nodded, on the verge of tears, grabbing for a bottle, any bottle, behind the counter.

The bicep was gauzed double this time with a little Saran Wrap for dressing. Jimbo helped Ricky hoist the sweater over his head. Before heading back out, Ricky blurted, "I need another favor, man."

Jimbo stopped in his tracks. He was afraid of this. Had a feeling it was coming.

"I need to borrow some money, bro."

"How much?"

"Enough to last me on Catalina...if you got it."

Jimbo reached under the cot and pulled out a cigar box filled with a stack of bills. As he counted it out, the image of that glorious sailboat blipped out of his mind. *Damn*. He was only five hundred short of the deposit.

"Fifteen hundred's all I got. I can loan you half."

"Shit, that's perfect. I owe you *big*."

"It's okay, man. I know you're good for it." He peered at his watch. "Sophie should be here any minute."

Varla was having her way with a Grey Goose bottle when they strolled back in. Mike and Doc were glued to the TV. The jukebox was silent, leaving the breaking news broadcast to echo throughout.

Jimbo said, "What's up, guys?"

"Someone got killed on the beach in Hermosa," Doc said.

"Jesus." He ran over to the tube with faux interest.

Ricky stood still, swallowed hard. He was met by Varla's scornful eyes.

She said, "It was Mick Gorso who got it."

Jimbo kept up the shock factor, asking for more details.

Varla wiped her eyes and went to grab her purse. The Deuce became the last place she wanted to be. Mike watched the interaction between her and Ricky as she stormed into the women's restroom. Ricky's face was green, looked like he wanted to hurl. Mike tried to stand up and regroup but the liquor had made his legs flimsy. He sat back down.

Jimbo tried to uplift the tragic mood with another round of shots. Varla emerged from the bathroom in a drunken rage, walking up to Ricky and slapping him hard on the cheek.

"And you know what that's for, don't you?"

Ricky turned away from her as everyone stared on.

"Yeah, you do." She swayed. "Well, I hope everything works out for you, Ricky. Have a nice life." She stumbled through the back corridor, not even acknowledging the rest of them.

Before anyone could speak up, there was a pounding at the

front door. Jimbo checked his watch: four fifty-eight. He scrambled for the key that unlocked the entrance. The TV news flashed again, now posting a picture of Ricky Fulton, suspected killer at large. Mike's and Doc's mouths dropped. Ricky ripped the TV from its socket, heaving it to the floor. Just then, a tight brunette flew through the front door and rushed toward him. Sophie. They met in warm embrace.

Mike pulled himself up from the stool, scenes from his career flashing before his eyes in kaleidoscopic fashion. A good collar might possibly get him back on the force. This collar here could clear his good name. Maybe? Maybe not. He shook out the cobwebs in his brain. Might as well find out. He reached into his jacket, pulled out the .38 and leveled it at the couple. Sophie gasped.

Doc said, "What are you doing, Mike?"

"I'm placing this *killer* under citizen's arrest."

Ricky's face boiled. He contemplated lunging for the gun.

Mike was having a hard time not seeing three of everything. He squinted for clarity. "Turn around, boy. Put your hands behind yer back!"

Jimbo could see Mike's eyes swimming and slunk carefully behind the bar. Ricky and Sophie watched the old man try to keep it together as Jimbo came up behind him with an empty gin bottle.

The last thing Mike said was, "Hold it now," before glass rained all over him, sending him face-first to the floor.

Ricky grabbed the gun and tossed it to Jimbo. "Thanks a ton, man. I owe you *waaay* big now."

Jimbo couldn't even form a response before they were out the front door. Wheels screeched up the highway. He and Doc just stared down at poor Mike, slack-jawed, snoozing one off like an infant on the dirty wood floor.

They eventually propped Mike back onto his stool, laying his torso limp on the bar. By the sound of his snoring, Doc knew he'd be okay, taking his pulse regardless, becoming a man of medicine again. Jimbo convinced him to naysay the whole ordeal, promising a year of free bar tabs. He also promised to turn on the old man if he talked, instilling the fear of a lengthy jail sentence for a stolen pharmaceutical distribution rap. They were just going to play it off like Mike passed out after a few more 151's, slid off the stool, and knocked his head on the floor—they'd picked him back up, of course. Just had to hope for the best now.

A few locals began to file in around six, laughing at the sight of a sleeping drunkard and harping about the news of the homicide in Hermosa. The sun spilled through the front door as Jimbo slung beers and Doc socialized, swilling Guinness as if the morning was fine indeed.

Mike got to grumbling around eight, propping his head up before feeling the pain shoot up the back of his skull. The locals pointed and chuckled. He surveyed the room, wondering what the fuck had happened. His gun was in the holster, a watery drink in front of him. Jimbo beamed a Cheshire grin from behind the bar. Before Mike could even ask anything about last night, some goof sitting behind him said, "Hey, ain't you that cop just got discharged for boozin' on the job?" The whole joint laughed even harder, creating a noise worse than giant cow bells. He stood up slow, stomach pumping with sickness. His mouth began to water. All he could manage to mumble was "Fuck all of you," before rushing on down to the head.

NOT EVEN A MOUSE

As tinsel dripped from every fixture, reflecting festive bulbs askew, the company cringed at each slurred syllable spat from Max's lips. If only his hoisted cup would keel, raining party punch into eye sockets, searing that sordid brain to an abrupt stop. So much for Christmas miracles.

Whispers clashed between employees as the rant took a breather.

"Solid gold—every year."

"'Tis the season…"

"God, what a fucking wreck."

"Somebody should really do something."

A nod bounced over a snowman tie, arm raising a cell. "I am—gettin' this toast for posterity." He sneered, "Classic Max. Watch it go viral."

They laughed into cups.

Max caught wind, tie slouching from the forehead, toast deflating. "Fuggit!" He chugged, ruby streams dribbling off the chin. A single burp roared at the sea of drone eyes, heralding triumph for a beat, ultimately barreling him toward the commode.

First stall didn't budge; bingo on door two. He took a knee and spewed a yuletide stream, tie dangling into contaminated waters.

"Max? You okay, buddy boy?"

The voice came from the first stall. He looked up at a man

and woman peering over the partition.

"I'm good, George." He headed for the sink. "What you guys doin'?" Through the mirror, saw the stall door swing. A grin crawled up George's face; the woman adjusted her blouse, steadying a mistletoe broach.

George approached. "How's the Sony account goin'?"

Max slurped cold water and pulled a hundred-dollar bill from out his pocket.

George held it up, letting fluorescent bulbs expose any flaws. "*Fuck*, this prop could pass on the street. Has the director seen these?

Max shook his head. "Just a prototype."

"Nice work. Can't wait to see the film."

Max took back the bill, knowing damn well how good it was.

George's hand shot out, displaying sharp white tablets. "Take 'em. They'll get ya back in the spirit."

Max popped four, dry. "Ups?"

"Nah—you're good though."

He plopped a hand on George's shoulder. "Thanks, man."

"Don't mention it. This luncheon blows. Happy Holidays."

A single nod told Max to get lost.

Jello stood back with the mop and admired his work. Checkered linoleum glistened throughout the shop, reflecting red lights strung across walls of hand painted flash. All stations were sanitized: steel tables wiped, trash cans emptied, supplies restocked for the next day's work—one after next. Place reeked of surgical gloves.

Soon he'd be scheduling his own clients, making money. For now, the apprenticeship was keeping him busy. Was hard enough getting a shop to even glance at his portfolio, let alone take the art seriously. Sonny saw something in him, never did ask what. He studied Sonny's station, admiring tubes and custom machines for shading or fine line. Proud stencils were taped up like fish scales, never discarded. His station, if Sonny gave him one, would be set up like this: a master of the trade.

He left the lights on, using the shop phone to call Mindy. Verizon killed his iPhone last week; same way the cable shut off—black magic. The year had been long, but next would be better. Had to. Life was riding on it. Mindy picked up.

"Don't hang up, baby. Just wanted to say Merry Christmas."

"Can't talk to him."

"Why not?"

"You know why. No support, no contact. Can't even buy him presents this year."

"I'm working on it, alright?"

"Yeah, right…working. Who the fuck leaves a perfectly good job when they got a wife and toddler?"

"That job was hardly perfect. Your dad fuckin' hates me, Mindy."

"So, you go an' give him another reason to? Just another idiot decision to add to the list."

"List?"

"You're serious right now? Where do I begin—trading in the Honda for a busted-ass guzzler—signing a five-year lease on an apartment I didn't even get to look at! Don't get me started on our credit."

"Okay, first off, you didn't have a problem with the Caddy until it took a shit—and I told you about the lease. Who seriously reads that fine print? Our place is vintage L.A., thought you'd love it—"

"I don't."

"What about Mrs. Topalian? Hate her too?"

"Of course not. Don't use the neighbor to rationalize your stupidity."

"Just saying—never would have met the woman if it wasn't for this apartment."

Mindy sucked a tooth. The old woman was a sweetheart, watching Buddy from time to time. Loved their young love. *Still…*

"Come on, babe—I'm tryin'. Quit drinking an' everything—focused on my work."

"You're not welcome over this year."

"The fuck am I supposed to do then? I'm gonna see my son on Christmas!"

"Shoulda thought about that before you done all this—forced us to move out."

"I didn't force you."

"Might as well have. Can only eat so much Ramen in one's lifetime."

"Can I see him tonight—bring him by the apartment?"

"Can't do it. We got midnight Mass."

"Jesus," came under the breath.

"That's right, *Jesus*—He's the reason for the season. Times like these, we take every blessing we can get. Least *He* shows mercy."

He choked back a *Christ*. Three weeks at her parents' and back to being programmed. He thought quickly. "I got Buddy some presents—just wanted it to be a surprise is all—like last year." He cringed. "Got something for you too."

"Bullshit."

"Think so?"

Her silence washed a smile: a tremendous feat.

"Well, we can't come over tonight."

"I know. How 'bout tomorrow?"

"We'll be opening presents all morning, so…"

"So, after that."

"Before Mom's dinner."

"Okay."

"Only for an hour."

"Okay—what time?"

"At night."

"When?"

"We'll be there when we get there."

"Merry Christmas, darlin'."

"Oh, you too, sugar plum."

Jello slammed the phone and went to turn off the remaining lights. He paused at the front window display. *Why even leave?* Shop was warmer than the apartment. He re-plugged the antique metallic tree, gazing at the life-size Santa beside it. Sonny bought it at a flea market because it looked demonic. Thing was taller than he was. He grabbed a candy cane off a limb, popped it in his mouth and proceeded to remove the dummy's jacket. Fit perfect, toasting the bones.

He sparked the storefront neon, peering outside. Boardwalk was void. Even beach bums had a place to go. He retrieved a tattered sketch pad, realizing that he'd filled the beast. Each page bled with paint markers or silver lead. *Don't feel like drawing anyways.* Wanted to relax. He pulled a television from under the front counter and rigged the box to life. Couldn't remember the last time he sat back and enjoyed a movie.

Two flies grimaced over cans of Olympia, sparking the young barmaid to spike the juke. They glared at the asshole seated by a tower of pints, crying like a preacher into his cell, hoping the drama got taken outside. Max didn't budge, plunging a finger into the other ear, yelling over Bowie. Barmaid shrugged, "Most wonderful time a da year, huh? You can keep it."

Max heaved another shot, body tingling from the meds. "I'm at a fuckin' bar, Bill. A shitty fuckin' bar in Culver *fuckin'* City, man. Why don't you call me?" The line went quiet. He wiped snot with a napkin. "What ya mean, 'kiss-a-death'? How will I screw everythin' up, Bill? *Oh*, okay. Whatever you guys think's *best!*" He bit a nail. "Meet me tonight—where Dad used to take us on Christmas? Come on—like old times…Why not? Look, I'm gonna pay you for that urn, all those flowers—when Dad—I was in a real bad place, alright? But—I got the money now, Bill. 'Member, last time I called, told you 'bout those investments? Well, they came through big, man—I mean, shit went back and forth for a minute—*but* I'm on top now. Listen, any amount you need..." Another sob swelled. "You should call me, man!"

The bartender dropped a receipt in front of him. "You're done."

"Wait a sec, Bill—what?"

She flung a dishrag over a shoulder. "You're cut off. Pay up, take those tears for a walk."

His jaw went slack, turning to the flies for support. Their mugs rang it home. "Sorry for the inconvenience, fellas. Talkin' to my older brother for the first time in five years over here—but I'll go. Don't wanna kill this perfect eve of Christ comin' out the pussy." He flung a hundred onto the bar. "Next round's my treat." Phone shot back to an ear. "Sorry, man. This bitch just eighty-sixed me—no way, I ain't done talkin'...Okay, well I can hear Donna yellin', so—hey, tell her I said, Merry—"

The call dropped.

He kicked through the front door, stumbling toward a vacant boulevard.

A cab dropped him at a liquor store in Venice. Loading short dogs of Cutty into a sack, the clerk's eyes never left the TV: some flick with Steve Martin, Santa and a transvestite.

"You know, they film this light outside here?"

Max dropped cash on the counter. "You don't say?"

"It vas pletty vonderful—to see it all happen."

"Well, look at you."

The clerk snapped the bill, eyeing intensely. "Velly crisp."

"Fresh out the mint."

"Ah, yes—new. Vell, Melly Clistmiss."

"Yeah."

He tossed the sack, lining his coat with clanking bottles, cracking one to his lips as waves crashed in the distance. A walk on the beach would be nice—then again, not getting mugged would be better. He peered back through the store window; clerk was sucked back into the movie. Max grinned.

Down the way, lonesome neon caught his eye. He approached the shop. Inside, a shirtless Santa greeted with evil eyes. Some dude had his feet propped on the counter, watching a TV. He knocked on snow frosted glass. "You open?"

The wad of cash in the guy's fist was thick as a tallboy. What was Jello to do? Never expected that response when uttering, "We're closed." Here was an opportunity that provided some experience along with monetary gain. Sonny was home with his family, rest of the crew wasn't expected before the New Year. *No one would ever know.* He scanned the boardwalk; no creatures stirring. Guy's glazed eyes helped the decision. He unlocked the deadbolt and swung the door. "Come on in."

"Thanks, man. Merry Christmas—name's Max."

"No problem. Jello—nice to meetcha."

They shook.

"Jello? The fuck kinda fruitcake name's that?"

"Ugh, just a nickname."

"Sucks for you."

"Not really. What can I do you for?"

Max approached the walls, admiring images of love, death and glory. "Nice shop. Lookin' to get some work—you draw all these?"

"No—not me personally. Ones you're looking at are from some artists who come through the shop. Those on the far wall were done by the great Sonny Bix—guy's a legend, owns this place."

Max gave them a glance.

"They're all done in watercolor too—pretty impressive."

Max shrugged. "Was lookin' to get something a little cooler."

"*Okay.*"

The TV caught Max's eye. "You know this flick was filmed right outside here?"

"Yeah—figured after seeing the hanging Venice sign. Shop's in the background too, few scenes."

"Alright, don't gotta break my ass, *Jelly.* Just saying."

"It's Jello. Sorry, didn't mean to be—"

Max pulled out a dog. "You mind?"

"Go for it." He watched Max take a generous slug, second guessing the decision. "So, what were you thinkin' 'bout gettin'?"

"Oh…" He burped. "Somethin' classy."

Jello reapplied the stencil for a fourth time.

Max studied its placement in the mirror, shirt off, paunch bulging. "Sure you done this before?"

"Tons a times. Neck's a hard area to, ugh, center the, um, thing there."

Max took another gander. "Spoken like a pro."

Jello met him with a forced smile, adjusting a masseuse table.

"Rather be sitting up, man." Max dangled a fresh dog and cracked it.

"We can do that. Whatever's most comfortable."

"Good."

As Jello wrapped a chair in cellophane, Max studied art engulfing the kid's hands, neck and head. "How old a you?"

"Twenty-three."

"Who does your work?"

"Sonny, mostly."

"Nice." He chuckled, "Maybe I should be waitin' for him to come in?"

Jello shot up. "Look, if you don't want the piece—that's fine. You been here for two hours already—"

"I want it—I want it. Just joshin', man."

Jello removed the Santa jacket, snapped on black gloves and sat.

Max adjusted on the chair, watching as Jello shook ink containers before filling drops into tiny red thimbles.

Jello punched the machine pedal with a toe. The *bzzzz* had Max jump. He laughed. "First time?"

"So what?"

"Sure you're up for this?"

"How bad could it be? You got 'em."

"Har-har." Jello regauged the machine's settings, checking the needle's rhythm, adjusting rubber bands around both coils accordingly. One hand applied Vaseline to Max's skin; other dipped the tip into some black. "Here we go, tough guy."

Max cringed at the initial tear, each carve feeling better and better. Endorphins gelled with booze, coursing the system into a dream state. After ten minutes, he was relaxed.

Jello's tongue turtled, in deep concentration. He focused on all those oranges and pork hides Sonny had him practice on. "So, what you do for a living, Max?"

"Work for a printing company off Culver—mainly studio stuff: billboards, posters, movie props."

"Not gonna get fired over this, right?"

"Who cares? Other shit jobs out there. Do what I want— they got a problem, screw 'em. Had our crappy Christmas lunch today."

"How was that?"

Max hesitated, reliving *the toast.*

"That fun, huh?"

"Buddy a mine fed me some downers."

"Oh yeah?"

"Shit made me all weepy. Didn't care for 'em." He sucked the bottle. *Fuckin' Bill—what a dick.*

"Hard liquor man, huh?"

"That's right. Don't usually drink though."

Jello took his toe from the pedal.

"Well, not in the past few months."

"Oh?"

"Was gettin' outta hand. Burnt bridges, all that good stuff. Got a hold on it though."

Jello watched him kill the bottle, wiping blood with a paper towel. "I hear that. Went on my own tear, few months back. Moderation's king."

"King a what?"

The machine hummed between their thoughts. Max broke the silence.

"Got plans for tomorrow?"

"You mean today, right? It's three in the morning."

"Yeah."

"Supposed to have Christmas at the in-laws', but ain't invited this year."

"Welcome to the club."

"Yeah, well—wife's supposed to bring my son over at night."

"Sounds nice."

"How 'bout you?"

"Oh, I dunno. Haven't decided yet."

"No wife an' kids—family plans?"

"*Pftt*—no invites to nothin', just a couple greetin' cards—ones got their heartfelt wishes already etched in 'em. A brother and three sisters—he's down in Oceanside, the girls are up in Seattle. Usually head to my oldest sister's every year—brother's comin' up with his kids this time. Already got my plane ticket but everyone thinks it's *best* for me to stay away. I don't get it, man. I'm the asshole or somethin'."

"*You*? Nah."

Max smirked.

Jello waited for flesh to stop jiggling, scratching his nose with the crook of a wrist.

"So, what do a couple assholes do on Christmas then?"

"Who said *I* was an asshole?"

"Figured—with your Christmas day unwelcomin' an' all."

"That's just 'cause I finally made a decision for myself. Quit working construction with her dad, pursued my dream."

"This?"

"Yeah. Always knew I'd survive on art, somehow. Want to be my *own* man."

"Nothin' wrong with that."

"Tired of fucking things up, you know?"

"Askin' the wrong guy."

"Just wanna make this happen—start over, support my family. They don't understand me's all. Takes a little time to get going in this field. Money for supplies, building clients—Sonny sees my talent. Owe a lot to that man."

"Greenhorn, huh?"

"Not exactly."

"This ain't your first go at it?"

"Ugh, no."

"Be honest, sport. Too late now."

"I've done hundreds a pieces, all damn good too...just not on a human."

"Ah, yes...that's comfortin'."

"Didn't want to scare you."

"Good thing, only gonna have this forever."

"Trust me, I got this."

Max chuckled, sipping the dog. "Oh, sure. Complete trust, comin' your way."

"Guess we're both poppin' our cherries tonight."

"You, me—Virgin Mary makes three."

They busted.

Max swayed in front of the mirror. "It's a beaut, I say—a goddam beaut!"

Jello found Max's drunkard slang amusing. "You dig it, right?" Hoped he didn't notice the kinks.

"A keeper, sir. Love what you did with the horns there—the hooves—impeccable."

"Yeah, freehanded that."

"My god, her tits are marvelous."

Jello cranked his spine. "Come back, lemme get a picture—then I'll wrap it. Be good to go."

Max posed for a pic, face contorted, muscles flexed. He fell back on the chair. "What's the damage here?"

"Say...three hundred?"

"That a discounted rate or somethin'?"

"Nope. Three hundo's fine—believe me."

"What does the *boss* bill?"

"Two-fifty an hour."

Max bobbed, eyes closed. "Well shit, son—I been here the whole fuckin' night." He pointed a finger. "Dammit—the asshole of dawn is afoot. Name your price, kid!"

Jello applied tape to the wrap on Max's neck; shaving an epileptic would've been easier. "How's five then?"

Max rose, fanning out his roll. Bills rained to the floor.

"I can't accept that. It's too much."

"Nonsense, my boy. You're a family man. Treat your clan on this fine Christmas morn!" He reached for another dog, face frowning upon the dreaded realization. "Rats...I'm dry."

"Want me call a taxi?"

"That'd be splendid. Come grab a drink."

"Can't. Not today."

The jolly slang stopped. "What—gonna leave me all alone on Christmas? I got nobody, man. Just did you a huge solid—"

"Told you, I don't want all that."

"I want you to have the money, man. Listen—I didn't fly the coop once you told me that you lied about bein' a—"

"I didn't lie."

"Whatever—said you got no place to be till later, right? Let's go catch a flick or somethin'. You were stuck in that other movie till I showed up—ruined it for ya. Come on, it'll be fun. Gotta have somewhere to be on X-mas."

"No theaters open today."

"Nah, I know a place."

"What movie?"

"I dunno—a good one. Guy I know's a projector at this revival house—plays an all-nighter every year for the die-hards. It'll be on the arm."

Jello tranced at all those crisp hundreds, knocking Mindy's

foul remarks to the back of the brain. *List?* Fuck her. She'd let him too, after seeing all that cash. *Got a few hours to burn.* Knew sleep wouldn't come either. He snapped off the gloves and headed to dial a cab.

In a damp alley, they traded puffs on a one-hitter. Jello ganked nuggs from Sonny's station; shit was cool like that. Might as well make this excursion interesting. *Indulgence is king on Christmas, right?*

Max craved more dogs but settled for the exotic twist on his bender. Felt like a tree fucker—hadn't smoked since high school. He pounded on the brick building's metal door. "He's here, man—spoke to him the other day."

Jello spouted dragon nostril smoke, wondering what the hell Max was up to; the busted marquee was clearly around the corner.

The door opened, revealing a wiry white kid, hair crazed over specs the size of hockey pucks. He shielded newborn sunrays and deflated upon seeing Max. Jello figured this must be how everyone greets the guy.

The film was already rolling. Max belittled the geek in whispers before showing off his neck. Jello overheard the guy say, "Amazing Christmas film," as he walked up a far aisle with caution, eyes adjusting to darkness.

A white ball bounced in the middle of the screen, getting larger as a narrator barked a smoker's tone. Jello leaned against a wall, taking in the oddity as the herb hit hard. Heart felt like a giant moth. Max rushed up the aisle, pointing out the best seats.

This bouncing ball was actually bright light at the end of a subway tunnel. Soon as the camera smacked it, the room burst white. Jello could see four shadowed skulls in attendance. Each was seated strategically apart, maintaining separate worlds as the narrator hypnotized...

You're alone but you don't mind that. You're alone—that's

the way it should be.

Max began to comment on the room of "losers"; Jello shushed him.

You've always been alone. By now, it's your trademark. You like it that way.

Max leaned over again. "Want anythin' from the snack bar?"

Jello shook his head, and Max vanished. One of the viewers turned with a look of disgust. Jello thought, *What a way for someone to spend today of all days*, then realized he too was now alone, the film his only refuge.

Time flew. Celluloid trapped their souls, burning the eyes, erasing all hurt. Afterward, they burst from the theater, clamoring under its marquee like boys marveling their first X-Men fix.

"Fuckin' fantastic."

"I know, right? Aren't you glad you came now?"

"That gun dealer with the pet sewer rats!"

"Yeah, he was in *Shock Corridor*, I think? Dug the ending too."

"Thanks a lot, Max. Really needed this today—just didn't know it, I guess."

Max smiled. "My pleasure." *See, Bill—ain't no* kiss-a-death. He fingered the plane ticket in his pocket, deciding on dark Seattle sunsets. *Flight isn't till later.* "Let's call a cab—grab that drink."

"Dunno 'bout a drink. Should get home and catch some *zzz*'s before the kid comes over."

"That ain't till tonight, man."

"Still."

"Come on. Least you could do is share one lousy beer with me."

"There's no place open this early."

"Oh, I got a place."

"You and your places."

"That's right."

Jello stewed. Thoughts of Mindy and Buddy in their Christmas morning grandeur poked the heart. "*One* beer?"

"That's it—on me. Then I'm out your life for good—promise."

Mindy blew on a steaming mug of cocoa, grinning as young Buddy frolicked amongst a sea of toys beside the tree. Mother heated up tamales and fried eggs while Father labored over instructions on how to build Buddy's new Big Wheel. She panned a few more times, grin falling; the scene began to ache.

She missed him.

Last year was perfect. He surprised them with all those gifts—that wonderful dinner. For weeks, he'd belted that they were broke. Sure, she'd asked Father to give him the bonus, but look how he used it: every cent on his family.

Thoughts trailed off into a future fantasy where all their problems seeped through walls; this was their home now, they'd become her parents, Buddy was now their grandchild. *Isn't that the dream? Why had I put in it peril?*

With every curse from Dad's lips, her gut twisted. *He should be the one fretting over the magnificent task.* She blew once more on the cocoa, drifting, longing. Her head began to tilt.

Mother's voice beckoned assistance, shattering the reverie for now.

The cruise rocked Jello to sleep. His mind reeled the final scene of that film, only this time he was the lonesome hitman, slaughtered off a dock into frigid waters. His teeth began to chatter.

Max paused from caroling and shook him back to life. "Get a load a that, man."

Jello peered at a Christmas tree lot, its *Fire Retarding* sign vandalized into hilarity. He sneered. Strange scenery flew through the windows. "The fuck are we, Max?"

"Redondo."

"*Redondo!*"

"Relax—you got enough scratch to get back to Venice." He

fingered his temples. "An Oprah-sized hangover's seepin' in. Gotta keep the party goin'. Look—we're here."

Taxi parked. Jello scanned the building; smooth art deco accents had it looking like a marshmallow. Sign above the entrance read *Eagles*. Max tipped the cabby big so he'd wait. Jello wondered how high up Max was at this printing company. *A total mess of success?*

They headed around back, entering a room filled with pool tables and shuffleboards. Flags draped down walls: Old Glory, POW MIA, Don't Tread On Me.

Jello turned to Max. "Thought you had to be a member to hang at a place like this."

"Used to. 'Bout to shut it down though—recession. Pops used to bring me an' my brother here when we were young. Always open on Christmas."

They pierced another doorway, revealing a modest-sized bar: wood fixtures, spider-webbed trophies—a blast from the past. Three seniors were huddled near a fuzzy Yule log, recanting tales on foreign soils. Jello's appearance brought the room to a halt. They slid onto stools. A bald barkeep slunk over: huge, maybe six-six. Fat fingers slapped the counter.

Max grinned. "Couple shots a Beam—Buds back."

Barkeep retrieved the order. Max turned to the older gentlemen, now staring full bore; their gold print hats featured carriers or planes. "Merry Christmas, fellas," was met by throaty grumbles.

Barkeep slid the hooch. "Start a tab? Cash only."

"Sounds good."

"The hell's on yer neck?"

"Like it?"

"Nice jugs."

Max turned to Jello. "Got another fan."

They clanked glasses and slurped.

* * *

One shot turned into six. Beer bottles cluttered. Jello saw another bourbon placed before him. *Last one.* He slammed the glass onto the counter and rose, legs a bit suspect. "Thanks for everything, Max—really appreeshate it. Gotta go."

Max's tented eyes nodded for the rest of his head. He slid a hundred onto the counter and gave Jello a monster hug. "One more...for da road?"

"Nope."

Barkeep swiped the cash and approached an antique register. He held the bill up to the light, squinting. Began to snap and smell it. His brow scrunched, grabbing a marker from the pen jar.

Max took notice. *Shit.* He patted Jello on the back. "Be right back—gotta piss."

Jello sat, head resting in both hands.

Barkeep scribbled on the bill and flashed it to the seniors.

Outside, tires kicked gravel.

A slap woke Jello from slumber; a bat thumping his chest urged undivided attention.

"Where's your butt boy, dickhead?"

"What's up?"

The discolored bill dropped before him.

"Think I wouldn't notice, huh?"

One of the seniors shouted, "Ain't in the bathroom."

Jello shot up, eyes bulging. Before he could take a step, the men had his arms cranked. Barkeep came around and turned out his pockets. Max's hefty payment splashed the floor.

"Motherfucker."

"Wait—it's not what you think!"

"Fuck're you—a mind reader? Mort—get the door."

"Max. *Maaaax!*"

Screams were snuffed by five hairy digits. They tossed him on the floor. *Max, you filthy bastard!* He flailed at first, ultimately cowering as kicks and blows delivered Christmas cheer. Between belts, Mindy's harsh words sang the soundtrack, a bloody festive jingle, roaring his pickled brain to mush. *Fa-la-la-la-la, la-la-la-la!*

Through the rear window, the marshmallow shrank with every block. Max stared intently, waiting for a sign, hoping Jello didn't take too many lumps. *Why did shit have to always be like this? From top of the world to the depths of hell.* Just a few hours ago, Jello was praising him—that movie. He took responsibility for *that* experience. Now this...*Should just bail, forget the whole shebang. What would a decent person do?* The answer brought a sour face. *Poor Jello.* Never meant any harm—just wanted some kicks. *Kiss-a-death! Kiss-a-death!* Couldn't face the kid but had to make things right—least try.

At a red, the cabbie craned for instruction.

"One more time."

They recircled the block.

Still nothing.

"Park across the way—down a bit."

Tires nicked a curb, engine idling under shadowy spiked palms. Only sounds came from seagulls thrashing a trash bin. Max whispered, "Come on, ya sonofabitch." The Eagles' front doors flew open. Max's stomach dropped as Jello fumbled down steps, grasping his torso, lurching up the avenue with a hamburger face.

"There a cab stand close by?"

"Down at the pier, block an' a half. Dunno if any'll be there today though."

Max fanned bills through the bulletproof partition. "Swoop that kid over there—take him wherever he says. If he gives you lip, tell 'im Max says, *Sorry.*"

"You got it."

He opened the door and shot behind a palm.

The cab sidled Jello. Max watched him spin around, looking for answers. Once the taxi launched, he punched air and headed toward the pier.

A cotton marine layer hovered the bay, reflecting soft notes of blue. Max sat on a bench, admiring glass waves, flawless till crashing into shards. He pulled out the plane ticket and eyed the taxi stand in the distance before tearing it in two. *Could get one thing right in this life.*

On the sand, fathers and sons zipped wetsuits, waxing boards for a Christmas sesh. The day was so young, so peaceful, so perfect; a fresh canvas for the rest of the world. Maybe it'd let him partake in the beauty? His limbs remained still, lips shut: a statue till the gods took notice. A delayed bourbon jolt washed a smile. *Couldn't help it.* His hand rose and caressed the smoky sea, careful not to corrupt even a derelict sailboat: the only present beneath his crooked little tree.

Rage simmered as Jello dabbed wounds with the hack's handkerchief. Penniless, his mind raced, dodging Mindy's scornful digs, forming a plan. Sleep weighed, woozy. He was shaken from a nod, cab driver snapping fingers.

"Don't fall asleep, guy. Got a concussion—might not wake up."

Jello grunted.

"Take you to the hospital?"

"Nah." Only one place to pull himself together. "Keep up Lincoln, turn left on Washington. Tell you where to go from there."

He fumbled the shop keys, bloody fingers turning each into wet goldfish. Rubbing alcohol seared every leak as he forged bandages with gauze and medical tape. Few more tokes on the one-hitter killed pain. Driblets out the ear caused minor alarm. Foster care had bludgeoned him worse.

He rummaged station cabinets and drawers for child friendly toys. A spectrum of fluorescent markers slid into a pocket. *What about Mindy?* The subconscious droned, *What about her?* He caught a glimpse in a mirror. Needed a fresh shirt. The merch counter only had pink girlie tees. He scanned the store, thinking. That evil Santa suit burned red hot.

Mindy's beach cruiser skidded to a halt out front of the apartments. Night air was crisp and mesquite. Windows down the block featured family snippets, warm and, for the most part, happy. She unfastened little Buddy from his bicycle seat and removed the giant helmet before locking their ride to a light pole. Her fingers wiped drool from Buddy's chin and adjusted his clothes to adult regulation. The resemblance to his father was remarkable; every glimpse, like the first time they'd met. He giggled as she lifted him toward the stars.

Complex hadn't changed one bit: trash lined the balcony of those co-ed dumplings, same unit blasted Coltrane, pool still milky. Sure, Mom's refrigerator was stacked and there was always a babysitter. But...she could have all this. A far door opened near the stairs. An older woman approached in a garish sweater-vest.

"Hello, Mrs. Topalian."

"Merry Christmas, dear." She bent down. "And how are you tonight, my cute little man?"

Peach nails clawed Buddy's cheek. His eyebrows gave alarm.

"On our way to visit Daddy."

The woman huffed. "He's not been well without you, dear. Just this afternoon he came stumbling in, causing such a raucous with all of this—well, you'll see."

Mindy bobbed Buddy on her hip, imagining the episode. "Yes, well—I apologize. It's been hard the past few weeks."

"Marriage isn't easy, my dear. Remember, love is always better than war."

"Of course."

"My Paul has been gone for so many years...We have such a small window to cherish our souls."

She nodded, leaning in for a peck. "Merry Christmas, Mrs. Topalian."

The woman's stare chilled the back of her neck as they ascended stairs, buzzing unit 314. Buddy gnawed on his fingers as Mindy craned an ear. Could hear shuffling inside.

The door flung open. Mindy was startled at first. Last thing in the world she expected was Santa Claus *ho-ho-hoing* with a fistful of candy canes. She smiled as he bent over to kiss Buddy. Jello's eyes met hers for a quick moment; Buddy stared on, quietly amazed. She handed him over.

The living room was bursting with ornaments. She approached the metal tree by the television, remembering it in the shop's window, then that scary Saint Nick. "Sonny let you have all this...Santa?"

"Just borrowing—for tonight."

She bent down to four presents underneath. Each was wrapped with construction paper, random doodles intricately drawn. She reached into her purse, pulling out a thin, rectangular box, and placing it amongst the others. "Mrs. Topalian looked nice today."

"Yeah, I told her you two were coming over."

"She was waiting for us."

Jello sat Buddy on the carpet. "We should open the presents, since you gotta go soon."

"We can stay awhile."

His beard shifted. "Buddy, you want Mommy to play Santa's helper?"

Mindy animated, clapping to retrieve a gift.

They both helped Buddy unwrap.

Her heart sank the moment she saw the coloring book, made from scratch. Every page was filled with wondrous animals, trains, planes and boats. Buddy lit up, markers in hand, spitting, smiling; same as earlier, amongst the new toys. "Your turn, Santa."

"You first."

He watched as she tore out a pink Sonny Bix tank top.

"You shouldn't have."

"Oh, it wasn't any trouble."

"Well, thank you."

"My turn." He cracked open the thin box. A chrome pencil glistened.

"Thought it'd be good for *work*."

"I love it, babe. How thoughtful." He paused, then pointed. "Got one more there."

"Don't know why, haven't been the greatest girl lately."

Her face perplexed after opening. A leather-bound notebook, every page overlapped with sketch upon sketch.

"First one I've filled so far. Wanted you to have it."

"It's beautiful—amazing. You've really gotten a *lot* better."

"Had my first client too."

"No way."

He grabbed their camera, showing the picture of Max's neck.

"Whoa. Nice cans." She squeezed his hand. "I'm so proud of you, babe." Her eyes fell to the floor. "I...I'm..."

"Me too."

They embraced, lips locked, before laughing at Buddy, doodling blue marker onto his forearm.

"Uh-oh."

"Wants to be like Daddy." Her fingers tugged his sallow beard.

Before he could stop her, the swollen jaw was exposed.

"Oh my God. What happened?"

"Nothing—it's nothing. Got mugged earlier—funny story."

"What...where?" She pulled of his hat: maroon bandages, eggplant knots. "We should go to the hospital!"

"No."

"*No?*"

"Looks worse than it is. I'm fine, baby—really."

She was trembling.

He kissed her again, pulling her close. "It's Christmas. Let's just stay like this, okay? Right here."

She wiped an eye, and they returned to Buddy, lost in pure joy.

Her body brought warmth, ear nestling back to his heart. He sniffed her hair. *Thanks, Max—for everything.*

ANGELS LIVE HERE

With open arms, Los Angeles welcomed another casualty on a brisk August morning, free of earthquakes or heat-sparked brushfires to swallow the City back where it belongs. A cardboard crate held a newborn at the steps of Firehouse 35, a brick box filled with idle heroes slopping mediocre Denver omelets. The knock was faint, inaudible over a Dodgers' pennant race argument. No one was sure just how long the child had been there; shrill cries bled before anyone took action. Regardless of how the baby boy came to be, the City had another son, and the heroes triumphed at another task: calling the proper authority who handled these burdens. Los Angeles named the child Jack and bestowed upon him a legacy...

On a scale from moon to gutter, Jack was cradled by clouds. Could hear birds chirp, smell flowers even. Life was simple again. Solid job, new apartment—beat slumming with all those halfway rats. Didn't even think of the stuff anymore. Hadn't dreamt of nerve-end tingles or the bitter taste of pharmaceutical bliss. No pain left to kill. On the up and up, one day at a time...for as long he could swing it.

Knotting the bow tie became easy. Could snap the sucker without a mirror. The last button on his black vest popped into place as he barged through the Dresden Room's rear door. Inside, a snapshot of Los Angeles' golden age: vintage dining, stiff drinks—live croons to send patrons past the stars. Art Deco accents and celebrity eight-by-tens welcomed him toward happy hour. Larry was adding vermouth to a shaker when he caught wind of Jack, eyes straight to his watch.

"Ten ticks early, dunce."

"I aim to please, gramps."

Larry grimaced, tossing napkins before a couple of wrinkled women. "See how the new kid talks to me." The ladies smiled. "Take over here, Jack." He leaned in and whispered, "'Rhoids are flarin'."

Jack let the duffer squeeze past as he wrapped on an apron. "Mindy workin' tonight?"

"Six to close."

The seniors caught wind of Jack's grin as he shook their martinis. The smaller one began to sing, "I'm in the mood for *looove...*"

Head wagging, Jack presented the women their cocktails. "This oughta loosen you sweethearts up."

"You got a fat chance, Valentino."

Jack smirked as a voice resonated afar.

"Greenhorn!"

Wiping a towel across the bar's nook, Jack took his time answering the call. "What'll it be today, George?"

"You tell *me*, rookie."

"George—I been here for four months, two days, an' three lousy minutes. How long I gotta sling you rotgut an' milk before I get a little love, old man?"

"Took Larry a stretch before I called the bastard by his first name."

"Ten whole years, huh?" Jack grinned, grabbing the Clan MacGregor. "Can make that, I think."

"We'll see, rube."

Larry returned. "Leave him alone, George. About to teach him how to water down the MacGregor's."

"You would, scum."

"Drink up, Georgie-boy. Them days a glory are wavin' behind ya."

George grunted, rattling the narrow glass up to chalky lips.

Jack surveyed the shelves to see what needed doing. The band would be on at nine, place filled by ten. He rolled up sleeves and juggled limes, welcoming the night's long hustle.

Jack taught himself to juggle at age seven, when he was locked in a woodshed for weeks, fed ravioli in cans, given a garden hose for water—and a small bathroom bucket: the penalty for poor grades or not making his bed...

Foster nightmare number three.

Mother was small, sweet and powerless. She'd call him Muffin or Jackie Pie. Father worked nights at the port, a man of simple tastes. Preferred fists to the belt (sometimes both). Jack imagined the pock scars about Father's face as being billowing corpuscles from a cold black heart; they bled evil. Nevertheless, sometimes the wicked were just so.

He made the woodshed home, hiding racquetballs and paperbacks in the walls whenever Mother watched her soaps. So much time was spent there since bruises could alert authorities, again. The days ached less and less; his body grew used to torment. Occasional wafts of breakfast sausage or pot roast became added pleasures; that and juggling in the dark.

Lost years there spent praying to angels.

A neighbor searching for a dog was his savior—at least from that house. Not from the pains of living. Not from the future.

An ice bucket balancing act had Jack's brow beading. He was graceful through the surging crowd, dodging hoisted drinks and gut-busting fellas. Felt like an old carny, contorted in a leotard with those damn spinning plates. Soon as he made it behind the bar, the crack of a wet rag brought a sting to his right buttock, sending both buckets crashing to the floor. Mindy's high-pitched squeal brought on a smile. He pulled a towel from his apron and said, "When you least expect it, girl."

She approached with a forgiveness hug, raven hair pulled tight into a baby ponytail, bangs nearly blindfolding. She wore the same threads as Jack, maybe a size larger. He welcomed the embrace, taking in the essence of her neck: Marlboro Lights, blueberry Smirnoff. He patted her soft ribs till she burst out his arms.

"Oh, man—did you hear who's playin' with Marty and Elaine tonight?"

"Nah."

"Blimpie Fisk!"

He humored. "No fuckin' way—who the hell's that?"

"What?" She craned, cracking a trio of Buds. "Hey, George—new guy ain't heard of Blimpie Fisk."

George's head raised up off the bar; a weed-shackled rose, stretching for sun. "What I tellya, Min—not a hope in the world for that rube."

She grinned. "Sorry, Jack—that's my bad. For a minute there, thought you had some class."

Larry shouted from beyond, once noticing he was the lone barkeep. Mindy jumped back to take orders. Jack followed suit, salvaging any uncompromised ice. Between pours he imagined what a man named Blimpie must look like. How had he never heard of the guy, never crashed into his howling brass beats? Couldn't lie to himself. As if he hadn't given up everything the past ten years to follow those crummy, little, jagged, chalky, pastel—pretty little devils. He noticed Mindy peeping him drift through dreamland; a lone middle finger had her chuckling again.

The first dose had him breathless. Janelle Tawdry's dad's place off Fairfax. Was her *idea—the corruptor. Hell, he wanted it too. Hadn't forgotten all the crucifixes. Every room: writhing corpses nailed for sin. Was only going to take one and see what happened. Janelle wasn't having it. If she was taking four, so was he. Moment the dry things scratched down his gullet, she was on him like tiger to prey (He always pictured Janelle versus gazelle.) Didn't have to mess with clothes either—both in the flesh on Daddy's queen size.*

Every element of that day, ingrained forever. A bar set in stone; a height Jack just had to chase. The warmth of a voluptuous brunette. Her scent, as he went down. Those lovely waves from out of nowhere, coursing the veins, prickling his skin with every slow caress. He drowned in her as she rode and rode, pills seeping him into a perma-daze with corpses gawking on all sides.

Stoolies barked over Marty and Elaine's vanilla croons; their upright bassist scowled as he bled before ingrates. Random conversations clashed with chords:

"That bitch wouldn't know a decent script if it cut off his dick!"

"I'm pretty sure he didn't give it to me, right—I mean, I'm like positive he used a rubber..."

"Nah, Leo's a mixologist now. Can't even drink beer with the guy no more."

Jack lingered, arms crossed, taking in the vibes of a lame Saturday night. Tried to relish Elaine's organ and Marty's raspy high-hat, at least till the next rummy needed their life force. Mindy was on ice; Larry—back in the can. Didn't notice the guy at first. So many of them hip fucks wearing porkpie lids, so Jack figured he was just another fresh-face phony. The narrow black case had him pegged. *Had to be.* Sat next to the stage, doffing his ivory cap to the entire band as he placed the tattered case upon a knee and *clacked* it open. A soft yellow glow washed the man's chocolate features, shining a halo around his brim. Jack leered at Blimpie's lips; of all the stories they could play. The horn glimmered once out its cage, panting like a pooch as it got caressed with a polka-dot rag. Marty and Elaine's last number sizzled to applause.

"Two highballs and somethin' fruity for the lady!"

Jack stood locked in a zombie gaze.

"Hey, buddy! Two highballs—one blood an' sand."

Jack snapped back, pausing on the customer before grabbing glasses. Ice crashed into the freezer behind him. He turned.

Beads of perspiration clung to Mindy's nose under huge emerald eyes. "Get a load, Jack. There he is."

Low times began to clot.

Jack stood at the rear of the chapel, trying to keep a low profile. Poor Mick. Everyone knew they were partying together that night. Why Mick? Why not me? They planned to kick together, show everyone, fuck the world. Jack scanned those in attendance, envious of their warm tears. The "party" coursing turned his heart into an iceberg. One by one, pews paid final respects before the lid was sealed forever. Jack tried blending into stained glass as the bereaved rushed out past him. Most didn't even glance his way. Few mothers mean mugged. Wouldn't be back here tomorrow, could barely stand it now. Just wanted to see Mick and make right—try to at least.

As the last mourners awaited their viewing, he slumped on an empty bench and fanned through a bible, uninterested in every word. Wished his last set of parents were here to help him through this. They'd cut communication once the stuff killed those college years. Began to nod off as he waited; came to whenever his chin nudged his chest. Shouldn't have doubled his dose; this pain kill was grinding him senseless.

A large hand shook his shoulder. His eyes drooped open to an elder in drab charcoal pinstripes.

"Son, the chapel will be closing now."
Jack wiped drool from his lip, frantically searching for Mick's
pearl coffin.
"The viewing's been over for an hour, son. Tomorrow's
procession begins at noon."
Jack rose, too weary for disgust.
Maybe partying would help?

The room turned to granite; Blimpie's lungs cut through every stone body, precisely sculpting with each blustered blow. The man's face could've paralyzed a blowfish. Marty and Elaine filled *bop-ba-ta* notes, softening the atmosphere for Blimpie to soar. And he did—a trumpeting angel, hovering on a cloud of beats. The horn wailed, blathering bliss from high notes to low, barking at the moon as if it were the only wailing soul left in Los Angeles.

Nobody ordered drinks but stood staring, pondering the magic act before them.

The lucky few.

Air was sucked from the room, vacuumed through Blimpie's brass. He burst breaths back at them, making everyone choke on sound. Mindy rested her head on Jack's shoulder as they stood on crates behind the bar, faces aching from wonder. Jack's stomach began to twist, realizing this was what it was all about.

Life.

The epitome of being; the splendor of selflessness. Everything he'd been missing for the past fucking decade. From high notes to low, then back to high again.

The trumpet blew for a full hour. One final rush of *BliDo-dE-bLAPs* unleashed the crowd into a riotous frenzy. Hands clapped blood out the fingernails. The piano tip jar exploded. Blimpie bowed, wiping his mouth with the rag, settling the trumpet back into its blue velvet cage. Eyes everywhere bugged from the sorcery.

Mindy poked Jack on the cheek. "How 'bout an encore? Shots! What you want?"

Jack's smile leveled. "I don't drink, hun."

Her shoulders deflated. "Hey, George. Found us the Holy Grail. New guy's the lone bartender in L.A. don't take the poison."

George bobbed on his stool, barely managing to shake his head, words too big a task this late an hour.

She swatted air, letting Jack know she was fooling. Not like she minded drinking alone. Rye overflowed a shot glass. She held it under Jack's nose, saying, "To a blossoming threesome: me, Jack an' the Blimp." The hooch bounced up and in.

Jack wished that alcohol agreed with him, if only to form another bond with this beauty. Wasn't like he got lost on liquor for years and burnt every bridge—just never cared for the buzz, couldn't straddle the line. His mind wanted to shout to Mindy every kaleidoscopic taste/tingle procured from his one true love. A worthless encyclopedia of medicinal madness. Instead, all that came out his mouth was, "I'ma go smoke."

Night wind bit at the cheekbones as he struggled to light a Parliament under the Dresden's crown of bulbs. Streets were dead, just a lone prostie cleaning grime out her nails on the corner. Heard the crowd inside grow wild, yet again. The door swung; Blimpie and his cage emerged, escorted out by a slow walk of the bass. Jack stood there, leering, trying to muster up words that articulated his thanks.

Not a chance.

Blimpie tipped his cap and said, "Do it to it, youngblood," before waddling down the block, heels clicking through shadows.

Jack went lax, coughing smoke once the legend plopped down at a bus stop. With the cage resting on concrete, Blimpie awaited the next slug to whisk him through neon wilderness. Jack turned to the door (innards still pulsing from the gig), then back to the bus bench (streetside serenity). He sparked another cig, marinating over the coolest thing he'd ever seen.

* * *

Thirty-five and barely alive. Skid Row by day; hot prowl by night. Friday the thirteenth.

Desperation delivered a fractured orbital and bruised jaw. Jack could only remember the heat off the patrol car's hood and three ominous words: suspect in custody.

Surveillance caught him breaking into a CVS. Hadn't figured the pharmacy to be secured by its own rusted gate. Took too long for just one pocketful of miracles. A silent alarm circus ensued.

"There he is!"

"I got him."

The baton cracked his skull as he scrambled down the diaper aisle, jarring his world back to the living.

An open and shut case: such was life.

Mindy's celebration shots had exceeded their intent. After counting down the register, Jack escorted her home (per her request). She giggled and joked with him as they sauntered up Hillhurst, moonlight sparkling gutter dregs, city nearly quiet with only a few speeding cars. Someone deranged began to howl in the distance. Mindy squeezed his forearm as they approached her building, an impressive structure with intricate brickwork. Could've doubled for a fire station. The first floor featured an overpriced Italian eatery. They climbed the stairs to her apartment, a narrow hallway keeping them close.

She had trouble unlocking the door. "Wanna have coffee with me?"

Jack played it cool. "Sure thing."

There wasn't any furniture. Jack stood in the living room, cigarette dangling from his lips as Mindy searched for the ashtray, which was buried beneath a mound of laundry. Thanks to the restaurant, a garlic stench was profound. Jack took in the scene. A busted TV held a stack of *Variety* in the corner. Fast food wrappers sat stuffed in a lonesome trash bag near a hot plate. Mexican candles were scattered throughout. He picked one up featuring a Day-Glo green Guadalupe.

Mindy tossed the clothes back into a pile. "I can't find it. Just ash in the candle."

"Which one?"

She smiled. "Anyone you like, Jackie *Pie*. Electricity got cut for a few days last week. My roommate couldn't hang—headed back to Houston. Took a few extra shifts for me to get it turned back on. The candles are from some photo shoot she did."

"Actor?"

"Director."

He blew smoke out the window before snuffing the butt.

"There's a record player in my bedroom, if you wanna throw somethin' on." She pointed to the mound of laundry. "I'm gonna change into peejays and fix the coffee."

Entering the adjacent room, Jack saw a crate of vinyl. An eighties-era turntable with wood-framed speakers sat beside it. Couldn't help but notice four blankets layered on the floor, functioning as a mattress. The walls held a few of Mindy's headshots: smiley, stoic, surgeon, superhero. Her clothes and shoes were huddled in an open closet. More vibrant candles and their stickered salvation greeted at every turn. A weeping Christ had him thinking of Janelle Tawdry.

Mindy's record collection was minimal but essential. There were two Blimpie LPs: *Live at the Strand* and *Do It to It!* The choice was obvious. As the needle scratched, he contemplated Blimpie's brief words, wondering if they implied something more than just a trademark greeting.

Do what to what?

The horn jumped full swing as Mindy entered with steaming mugs. Her pajamas consisted of flannel pants and a black Frolic Room T-shirt. Jack tried not to stare at her stubby white toes, each nail painted turquoise. She handed him a mug.

"It's instant but I like it."

"Hard not to love anything *instant*."

She placed her mug atop a speaker and bent down to light candles. He watched as she crawled on all fours, ass twitching to the beat of the brass. Noticed she wasn't wearing a bra.

Her arm brushed his thigh as she reached for one final light. The pressure sent shockwaves up his spine. She rose, snapping her fingers, room aglow in a spectrum of colors turning the walls into stained glass. Jack thought of that chapel, then Mick's grey corpse. He shook out the image.

She pointed to the blankets, her skin cast in hellfire red. "Come down."

Jack slowly sat atop the blankets, careful not to splash any of his coffee.

"You know what would go perfect with this record?"

He shrugged.

"Pot."

"Pot?"

"Weed—you smoke right? Don't tell me you're an all 'round goody two-shoes."

He gazed up; the contours of her breasts forced a swallow. "Of course."

"Be right back."

Jack expelled a faint puff as she bounced from the room. He sparked another cig, sucking monster drags. Could hear a soft tapping in the other room. *Probably knocking resin out a pipe.*

Mindy hollered, "Take your shoes off—get relaxed."

Soon as he removed his boots, a black cloth flew into the room, nearly landing on a candle. He moved it, making sure it couldn't catch fire.

Firemen.

He looked at the cloth in his hands: *Frolic Room*, emblazoned in white. She stood in the doorway, lopsided breasts speckled with freckles, holding a mirror harboring six meaty white slugs.

* * *

Ambrose Avenue, Los Feliz: fourteen months shacked up with Hollywood's crestfallen. Lamest shit ever, although Jack enjoyed living outside a cellblock. Hadn't made any friends though; too wary of poor influences on his newfound sobriety. His roomie was an ex-pro surfer named Duff. Decent fellow, like himself, stricken by the fever of unattainable highs. Jack had dabbled in everything by now but only one dose made him weak. Duff was the opposite; he danced with speed, coke and heroin—simultaneously. He'd tell Jack about his plans once out the house for good, getting lost across the globe, searching for the perfect left. Duff's words were all he had; Jack could tell by the guy's eyes that he was helpless on the outside, too seduced for tranquility, too wild for surf. Jack worried about being the same; forever trapped halfway.

The days drifted slowly; chores and paperbacks to stew the brain. Three times a week, a counselor would break down his habits, set goals, create dreams. Jack would eventually help troubled youth upon the completion of the program and his counselor's consent. Nights were worse: sobs and screams from tormented tenants. Between the tasteless meals and the stench of communal living, reality pounded dust out the walls. On Jack's final morning, Duff pried for details on his fresh new beginning.

"Dunno, man—honest. Live one day at a time, see what comes my way. Gotta find an apartment, then job hunt. Got a few decent leads out the Weekly. *They said if I can hold my own for six months, they'll begin training me for youth mentorship and motivational speaking—that's the end goal. Just anxious to be a part of something, you know? A neighbor—a coworker—a* somebody. *Feel hopeful once again. If I can help anyone avoid the choices I've made, maybe all the pain wasn't in vain."*

Duff's hand clobbered Jack's shoulder. "What pain, bro?"

Jack smiled. "Exactly."

Mindy handed him the tray, kicked off her flannels and sat

down beside him. "No pot—but I found something better. Strip for me, Jackie."

Without blinking, Jack slackened the bowtie and popped buttons. His mind raced: *Coke—never had a problem with coke.*

Mindy snorted a line, biting her bottom lip.

Little yay'll be okay. No biggie.

He steadied the mirror on his palm. The record needed a flip; calm scrapes made the room an outer realm.

Do it to it—right, Blimpie?

Instantly, as the powder smacked his brain, all was kaput. No more cradled by clouds. Kiss the job goodbye. So much for being *somebody*—helping anyone. *Who am I fooling?* "This isn't coke."

Mindy placed the needle to the Blimpie B-side and grabbed the mirror, sniffling. "Nope—Oxy." She pulled an amber vial from out her pajamas as proof.

Jack closed his eyes as familiar tingles took hold. He relished every surge advancing his system, every bitter drip biting the throat. The world became soft as Mindy's curves.

She gave back the tray.

Jack attacked final rails.

Mindy placed the mirror aside and grabbed his hands. They gazed at each other's bodies, almost dreamlike as their blood charged in unison. In their chapel, Blimpie's brass was the organ. Before Jack could make a move, Mindy pounced, slamming him onto his back.

Janelle versus gazelle.

Their tongues slithered as Jack relived that first dose. Mindy rode and rode, radiating a fiendish aura. Candles wept over his fall; writhing corpses returned as righteous voyeurs. Gone were foreboding thoughts of his miserable life. He succumbed to the moment, the epitome of *his* being. Everything life had forsaken the past year plus—back in spades.

A final rush of *BliDo-dE-bLAPs* carried them to climax.

Jack smiled, grunting through bliss, the heart a live grenade.

A legacy fulfilled; a saga continued...
From high notes to low, then back to high again.

ACKNOWLEDGMENTS

A big thank you to Eric Campbell, Lance Wright, Chris Rhatigan and the team at Down & Out Books for believing in this collection. *Beneath the Black Palms* would never have been possible without the many publications that also believed in my work over the years, including Todd Robinson and Allison Glasgow (*Thuglit*), Anthony Neil Smith (*Plots with Guns*), Steve Weddle (*Needle*), David Cranmer (*Beat to a Pulp*), Jennifer Jordan (*Crimespree Magazine*), Rusty Barnes (*Tough*), Cody Sisco, Allison Rose and Gabi Lorino (*Made in L.A.*). Many thanks to Nat Sobel and his staff at Sobel Weber Associates for helping shape this collection in its early stages. To my family and friends, all your love and support is greatly appreciated. To Jenny Jay, T & C, for making my heart full. And lastly, to Los Angeles: the muse, the horror, the inspiration at root in each of these tales—a final cheers to your loveless gutters.

Photo Credit: Melinda Sanchez

NOLAN KNIGHT is the author of *The Neon Lights Are Veins*, a fourth generation Angeleno and former staff writer for Los Angeles' Biggest Music Publication, the *L.A. Record*. His short fiction has been featured in various publications including *Akashic Books, Thuglit, Crimespree Magazine, Shotgun Honey, Tough* and *Needle*. He lives in Long Beach.

On the following pages are a few
more great titles from the
Down & Out Books publishing family.

For a complete list of books and to
sign up for our newsletter,
go to DownAndOutBooks.com.

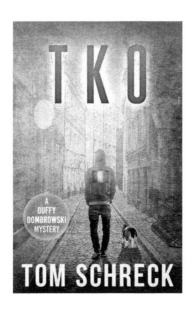

TKO
A Duffy Dombrowski Mystery
Tom Schreck

Down & Out Books
May 2022
978-1-64396-282-5

After twenty-five years in prison for murdering a couple of cheerleaders, a quarterback, and the class president, "Hackin'" Howard Rheinhart gets discharged. His case is assigned to Schlitz-drinking, Elvis-loving social worker and pro boxer Duffy Dombrowski.

Soon, local high-school VIPs start showing up dead and Howard is nowhere to be found.

Swing Gang
A Vince McNulty Thriller
Colin Campbell

Down & Out Books
June 2022
978-1-64396-268-9

Titanic Productions has moved to Hollywood but the producer's problems don't stop with the cost of location services.

When McNulty finds a runaway girl hiding at the Hollywood Boulevard location during a night shoot e takes the girl under his wing but she runs away again.

Between the drug cartel that wants her back and a hitman who wants her dead, McNulty must find her again before California wildfires race towards her hiding place.

Snake Slayer
Rob Pierce

Down & Out Books
August 2022
978-1-64396-271-9

Three criminals on the run, not just from the law but from other criminals. Two of them are lovers, the third her former lover. Where does love lie, except in the grave?

If you liked Pierce's *Vern in the Heat*, you're going to love *Snake Slayer*. And if you didn't read that one, strap in for the ride.

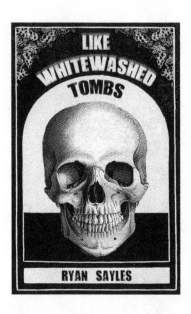

Like Whitewashed Tombs
Ryan Sayles

Down & Out Books
August 2022
978-1-64396-272-6

A bloody liquor store robbery.

Two diverging police partners. One is haunted by the pain of being widowed and God's request of him. The other is stalked by adversaries both spectral and all-too real.

Their already messy lives become further entangled together as redemption slips farther away.